ARNOLD
ETHON

— *and the* —

LIONS *of* TSAVO

A.P BESWICK

Clementine
Publishing

For information contact :

info@apbeswick.com

http://www.apbeswick.com

Book and Cover design by G. Veintimilla

ISBN: 978-0-9559-0392-2

First Edition: December 2019

Clementine
Publishing

Bio

Born in Blackburn before being raised in St. Annes, A.P Beswick always enjoyed creating stories and comics as a child. He is a registered mental health nurse as well as an author and he lives in Oswaldtwistle with his wife Sarah and daughter Etta. He also has another daughter Libbi and son Connor.
Arnold Ethon and The Lions Of Tsavo is his debut novel.
Visit www.apbeswick.com

Acknowledgements

Special thanks to Rachel for being the first person to test read this book. Thank you to my beta readers whose feedback has been crucial in the development of this story. To my editor Victoria, thank you for taking a chance with me and aiding me on this journey. Finally, to my wife Sarah and children Libbi, Connor and Etta, thank you for motivating me in everything I do.
I am lucky to have you all in my life.

Arnold Ethon and the Lions of Tsavo

Chapter One

Arnold gasped as the freezing cold air engulfed his lungs, instantly stealing his breath. The sharp, stinging sensation was initially uncomfortable, forcing him to take rapid short breaths just to take in enough air. After a few moments, he managed to gather himself enough to allow his breath to return to a steady, rhythmic pattern. He felt himself begin to relax as he became accustomed to his surroundings. He thought back to a few years ago when he was on a camping trip with the Cub Scouts. "In through the nose and out through the mouth," he told himself, recalling the advice he had received about surviving in the cold, not realising back then that he would actually find it helpful one day. Once he adapted to the cold, he was able to take in the mesmerising view. He looked out with a steady gaze, taking in all he saw. The fields below him were illuminated brightly by the haunting crescent moon above, making the adjoining fields look like a complex patchwork quilt. The moonlight also created a soft shimmer that made the grass look as though it was water. The trees moved in a synchronised motion as though they were dancing; their branches and leaves swayed gracefully backward and forwards as if being guided by a choreographer. Nature's very own ballet was a beautiful sight to behold.

His momentum steadying, he slowed to an almost complete stop but then suddenly felt as though he was going to fall. An overwhelming sense of panic engulfed him as he felt the fierce force of the wind pushing against him; nature's choreographer had changed the pace and Arnold needed to respond accordingly. He knew he needed to let the wind pass before he could move on but the icy chill that engulfed him felt as though it was touching every inch of his bones; it was a coldness he had never experienced before. He needed to persevere and ride the incoming gust of pressure generated by the ferocious wind, so he stretched his wings out as far as he could and tilted them at an angle to ensure the uplift from the wind steadied him. He was very aware of how easy it would be to lose balance and plummet like a rock to the hard, unforgiving ground below. This was an art form; the wind was a natural force and could not be tamed by anybody. He rode the breath of the wind rather than fighting against it, using it to his advantage. The force of the wind made his feathers vibrate against him violently, making it harder for him to focus. He just about managed to keep his wings in position and maintain a gliding stance.

Arnold maintained this focus until the relentless wind subsided, its crescendo coming to a head meaning that he could now relax and look at reaching down towards ground level. He changed his position again, gliding downwards at a steady pace to reach the patchwork fields below. Landing on a large branch of an old oak tree, he shook himself to bring all his feathers back into shape and he couldn't help but feel as though he must have lost a few of his feathers from his latest experience of night flying. He was still getting accustomed to this; he did not even know what he was, but he had a strong feeling that it was only a matter of time before he found out for certain.

"What on earth are you on about Arnold?" Arnold's dad, Arthur was sat across from the dinner table, his wrinkled forehead giving him a rather puzzled look whilst biting into his marmalade on toast. "Is this another one of your dreams?" he asked. The pair sat at the beechwood table eating breakfast, Arthur pushing his slightly greying, quiffed hair back as he spoke. Music was playing down the hallway from the kitchen where his mum was making their lunch. Arnold could hear his mum singing along to At Last by Etta James; it was one of her favourites. The smell of slightly burnt toast also filled the air, as it had been left in the toaster for slightly too long due to his mum being a little distracted by the song on the radio.

"Yes, it was". Arnold was making his way through his breakfast cereal, making a mess. His dark, unkempt hair needed some attention before he headed off to school. Arnold's lightly freckled face focused intently on his dad as he wanted to describe every detail he could, his dark brown eyes unmoving. He sat perched at the end of his seat, rapidly tapping his foot on the floor which began to make the table rock. Arthur wasn't giving Arnold his full attention however, as his eyes drifted over his newspaper.

"Honestly, Dad. It felt so real - like I was actually flying through the sky!" Noticing his dad's disinterest, he felt a wave of disappointment drift over him as Arthur appeared utterly uninterested in what he was trying to explain to him. "Are you listening to me?" Arnold snapped, feeling a rush of temper come across him, his voice slightly raised.

"Sounds good, son" Arthur murmured, seeming somewhat distracted. He lowered his newspaper gazing over the top, his glasses sliding to the bottom of his nose. He sighed loudly as he turned the page, the bold letters reading "The Oswald Advertiser". Underneath was the heading 'Menial uprising in London – Chichen will not change stance'. Arthur sat staring at the paper, concerned by what he was reading.

Arnold's mum came in from the kitchen. Her mousy brown hair tied up into a bun, she was already dressed for work in her light blue polka dot dress uniform. Her thin frame beneath made it very clear who Arnold took after. She began cleaning up the breakfast table. "Arthur," she admonished gently, "Arnold is trying to talk you about his dream". She shook her head at his attitude which brought a smug smile to Arnold's face. "It's about his dreams and you need to listen to what he is saying".

Realising how ignorant he had appeared in front of his son, Arthur made a fake coughing noise and folded up his newspaper, lowering it to the table and placing it next to the blue and white ornately decorated side plate which still had on his half-eaten marmalade on toast. "Sorry Arnold, what were you saying? It's just that there some artefacts were stolen recently, and it looks as though a group of menial fanatics has taken responsibility for it." Menial was the term used for somebody who couldn't harness any power from a spirit beast. They were seen by many in society as weak as they were unable to demonstrate any worthwhile talents as a result of not having a link to the spirit world.

It was obvious to everyone that it would have been menials that had stolen artefacts in London as it was only menials that seemed to show an expressed interest in them. Some of these artefacts had the potential to grant the bearer special talents which, to them, made them equal to those who gained talents through their spirit beasts.

"Do you think it was a menial?" asked Arnold.

"More than likely is, I mean who else would want to pinch an artefact?" Arthur responded.

"I would."

"Pardon?"

"If I was a menial, I would want to steal an artefact. It must be horrible not to have a spirit beast - doesn't even bear thinking about." Arnold was being deadly serious. His greatest fear was that he would be a menial which would absolutely devastate him, given the fact that he dreamed of working for the Chichen as his dad did. Unfortunately, to be a part of the Chichen you needed to demonstrate both spirit beast and talents to be able to join, and you had to be eighteen. You could not apply to join it; you had to be invited and invitations were rare given that you had to demonstrate acts of bravery to be recognised. Arthur had been in the Chichen since he was twenty and had spent his adult life protecting the local community of Oswald from those that wish to use their talents to cause harm or distress to others.

Arnold had always lived in Oswald, an old industrial town in the North of England. Back in the day it was a hub for coal mining as well as playing a key part in the industrial era in the early 1900s. The last of the coal mines had been flooded and sealed up over twenty years ago but many of the original mine entrances could still be seen. Oswald was now like most other towns with schools, local shops, butchers and - in Arnold's opinion - one too many bakeries. The town's claim to fame was that it was home to the world's largest pear drop which was on display at the old sweet shop inside the local factory mill outlet. Every day, wave upon wave of day coaches filled with people wanting to visit the sweetshop and all the other shops inside the old mill would descend on the town. The rest of the factories within Oswald lay dormant, these industrial graveyards a constant reminder of the dominant trade that once ran through the very veins of the town.

"I keep having dreams that I'm flying, dad. That's got to be a sign that my spirit beast is going to be a bird of some kind?" Arnold continued to press his dad for a response.

"Possibly, some people are said to have vivid dreams where they are an animal and for some of those people, that is the animal that has manifested as the spirit beast inside of them. It is quite rare Arnold, so maybe don't get your hopes up too much," he continued. "You also know that bird spirit beasts are pretty rare. Try not to rush this son; when your body is ready it will happen. I can assure you of that." His dad looked at him and realised he was never going to talk him out of his impatience. "You are going to go through changes. You may become quicker or stronger or have better reflexes and all that is going to depend on the spirit beast that you have inside of you. If you have a strong enough connection to your spirit beast you may be able to summon it one day as I can but it is not the be-all and end-all." Arthur took another bite of toast, leaving a trail of crumbs between his plate and himself.

"I need to be able to if I am to be a Doyen like you." For as long as he could remember Arnold had wanted to be a Doyen, protecting people from others by using his spirit beast. This is what Arnold believed to be his destiny.

"You're nearly fifteen now so before long you will know exactly what your spirit beast is. As I said, don't rush it. You can't join the Chichen and become a Doyen for a good few years yet, so for the time being go and enjoy being a kid. Trust me when I say being a Doyen is not as exciting as you think; crime is at the lowest it has been for a long time and that is because of our presence." Arthur looked across the table at his son's slightly crestfallen face and smiled gently. "I know you want to know what your spirit beast is and that's completely normal at your age". He took another bite of his toast, which made a loud crunch as he bit down, forcing some of the marmalade to push up against his dark greying moustache. Arnold chuckled at this and nodded at his dad to indicate he had marmalade on his face. Arthur quickly brushed it off before he picked up his newspaper and began reading again.

As Arthur finished his toast off there was a brisk knock at the door. It was an assertive knock that implied that it was someone familiar calling round.

"That will be your friend, Arnold" his mum called from the kitchen. "Time to head for school." Arnold stood up to leave the breakfast table. He was of a slim build along with the requisite adolescent gangly limbs. He had simply not filled out yet, something else that Arnold could not wait to happen. He grabbed his bag and coat from the hallway which was hanging off a hook as his mum handed him his lunch box. He headed to the dark green door, grabbed the handle and swung the door open. It was quiet outside as it was still relatively early, the sun was slowly rising meaning that the sky was still a greyish pale colour. The birds could be heard singing their morning songs, and a gentle breeze was in the air, just enough to ensure that a coat was needed. The ground was wet with the overnight showers; small puddles littered across the road and pavements just waiting for an over-zealous car driver to drive through and soak them.

"O'rite." Stood there in front of him was his best friend, Otto. Otto was a stronger build than Arnold as he was more athletic in stature. He was also slightly taller, but then he was also a few months older. He shook his head to clear his slightly long, brown tangled hair from his face. Otto had a naturally dark, tanned skin, which at times could make Arnold appear as though he resembled Casper the friendly ghost in comparison.

"Morning Otoronco," Arthur called from the dining room. Otto rolled his eyes and laughed.

"Please just call me Otto, Mr. Ethon," his northern accent appearing well-spoken like he had been rehearsing these lines. Otto often had to ask people to refer to him by his shortened name.

"I don't think your mum and dad would appreciate that!" Arthur's laugh could be heard from the dining room as he walked out and waved in Otto's direction, before walking into the kitchen with his bread crumb laden plate.

It wasn't that Otto hated his name. After all, it ran in his family; it was his grandad's name which he felt honoured to have been given. Otto found the name too long-winded and old fashioned which was why he liked to shorten it to something that he felt was more socially acceptable. This was much to his parent's dismay who often reminded him of how important his name was to their family. The Redburn family had a long history in Oswald that went back before the coal mining era. Otto's Great Grandad had worked his way up from being in the mines all day, every day to eventually being a foreman. Otto still resided in the old foreman's house which was the largest of the terraced houses that sat in the middle of his street. This had been handed down from his Great Grandad and then down to his dad and now he lived there with his parents and his five-year-old brother Tipu. Otto's dad was in the process of petitioning for the old coal mines to be re-opened to bring some much- needed cash flow into the town. As local mayor, he had more sway to achieve this as he had had in previous years.

When Otto wasn't at school, he spent a lot of time helping his parents with his younger brother who had autism; it was tremendously important to him. As a result of the serious role he had at home when he wasn't there, he liked to act the clown which was something that Otto did very well.

Much to Arnold's jealousy, Otto's spirit beast had begun to manifest itself. It was still in the early stages, but Otto's athleticism had improved since his fifteenth birthday, just a couple of months ago. The Redburn family had a history of their spirit beasts being in the category of the big cats. His dads was a lynx and his grandad's was a snow leopard meaning that Otto believed his spirit beast was going to be pretty epic. It was quite rare to have such similar spirit beasts within a family and most considered it simply a coincidence. However, the Redburn family had always had feline spirit beasts guide them through life and they considered it their legacy. When spirit beasts were linked through family blood this was known as Agnates.

Arnold shouted goodbye to his parents and set off down the road towards the school with Otto, avoiding the puddles that had formed on the pavement in a motion not too dissimilar to hopscotch. Arnold and Otto had been friends for just over a year. They had never really spoken to each other much at school as they were in different forms, but one day the two were paired up in PE and soon found out that they had a lot in common. This was mainly around comic book superheroes and the movies that these characters were in.

"You decided what you want to do for your birthday?" Otto asked. Arnold didn't have a large circle of friends meaning a party was out of the question.

"Maybe just head to the cinema?" he replied, looking at Otto for assurances that this was a promising idea. There were a couple of films that had come out recently that he would like to see.

"Sounds good."

Arnold and Otto continued their usual walk to school, across the sports field and through a ginnel that led past the local Chichen. The Chichen was where Arthur worked; it was also where the local Doyens - who were tasked with keeping the local town safe – were based. This was where the Doyens honed their skills through training and learned to truly master their inner spirit beasts. The building held a library full of literature about the ancient ways that were only accessible by those entrusted with them.

"One day, my spirit beast is going to be etched into this building," Arnold said, making the statement with pride as he gazed up at it. The bright sky behind the building made the grey stone shine as if a sheet of glass covered it, making it seem even more breathtaking. He wanted to be a Doyen so badly; it was all Arnold thought about lately even though it was just over another three years before he would be able to join.

"Not like you to mention that," teased Otto.

"Well, it will be."

"Don't you think you need to have a spirit beast before you can join? You haven't even begun to show signs of your spirit beast yet so let's face it Arnold – you're some way off becoming a Doyen," Otto chuckled as he continued to tease his close friend.

"Wow - don't hold back," Arnold replied, Otto's comments causing him slight irritation. He was completely right, however. He was such a long way off being able to train as a Doyen. Arnold put his hands in his pockets and kicked out at a small stone that sat on the floor which skimmed across the pavement before coming to a stop on the other side of the road.

"Sometimes, you need to be realistic with these things," Otto continued, a playful grin across his face. "Come on, we are going to be late if you stand here daydreaming all day." He looked at his watch. "Mr. Higgins will kill me if I'm late to form again. Last one there is a Menial!"

Otto set off running up the street at speed, hurdling past the puddles on the floor with ease. He even vaulted a wall with minimal effort as he took a shortcut to get to school on time. Arnold couldn't help but laugh to himself. For someone so quick, Otto was always late or arrived at the last minute, something he was on report for at school. He was happy for Otto as he had very recently become faster. A LOT faster. This was a sign that his body had begun to link to his spirit beast, and it had started to manifest itself within him. He couldn't help but feel a little bit jealous as Otto had started showing the physical signs which he was still waiting to experience. Until a spirit beast had fully manifested though it would be anyone's guess what it's identity would be. All they knew is that teenagers would begin to show attributes linked to that animal at around fifteen years old. In Otto's case, his speed had increased dramatically, combined with his ever-improving agility. Arnold and Otto's theory was that Otto would be following suit with the rest of his family and his spirit beast would certainly be in a feline form. Arnold set off running after Otto also not wanting to be late, but it felt like an age for Arnold to catch up to him as Otto was so much quicker. Arnold wasn't even a fraction as agile so he couldn't vault over the wall like his friend had, choosing to run around it instead.

Arnold caught up to Otto at the entrance of their school, but this was only because Otto had stopped running and was waiting for him to catch up. He was leaning against the entrance gates to the school, a smugness emitting from him. He was always going to win given his newfound talents and that heavily tilted the scales in his favour.

"Yeah, coz that was a fair race!" Arnold puffed as he caught his breath.

"Don't be so bitter! You never know, you might even beat me one day," Otto smirked.

"The sooner the better," Arnold laughed. "You're becoming unbearable!"

Chapter Two

"I had another dream that I was flying last night," Arnold panted, as he pulled up next to Otto, breathing heavily to get his breath back. "It felt so real, I could honestly feel the cold air against me."

"I'm guessing you left a window open." Arnold shook his head slowly at Otto's continued attempt to tease him. "I'm all ears," Otto said, realising that he had just about got away with that last joke at Arnold's expense. Arnold and Otto continued through the wrought iron school gates, with Arnold explaining in as much detail as he could about the vivid flying dream that he had the night before.

Arnold made it through the first half of the day, somehow surviving the perpetual boredom that was school. It was only Monday, so he knew he had a full week to get through before the weekend. As school days went, it was up there with the more laborious ones; maths, followed by physics made the morning an extra special mind-numbing one for Arnold. He had not been paying attention in maths today and had spent the lesson colouring in the alternative squares that filled his math book. He chose to do that rather than the revision the class had been requested to do by the substitute teacher, a man who was not exactly an advertisement for getting into the teaching profession. Arnold felt as though his mind was going into a dark hole as he etched his pencil into the small squares, making a small scratching noise in the process. All he could think about was that vivid dream, the sensation of flying and how real it felt. He wanted this to be a sign of his spirit beast so badly. He continued to fill in the squares, increasingly unconsciously; colouring in the squares faster and faster, pressing down harder until eventually the end of his pencil broke, snapping Arnold's attention back into the room.

"Have you worked out your frustration Ethon?" The substitute teacher calling him by his last name, drawing attention to the fact he wasn't doing his work. He had been oblivious to how feverishly he had been sat scribbling in his book. Leaning across the rectangular table, he opened the maths book and finding the page he needed, began to take notes on algebra.

"This is pointless." The words came out of his mouth without him even realising.

"Pardon?" There was a snigger from some of Arnold's peers, surprised by this uncharacteristic outburst.

"Nothing, Sir." Arnold began silently writing his revision notes, not that any of it was sinking in as again, all he could think about is his spirit beast and what this would be. He would struggle with these lessons on a normal day but today his dream was taking up all the mind space that he had. He knew that it was only a matter of time before his spirit beast manifested but he was beginning to grow frustrated at waiting for a physical sign. He wanted the changes to happen to him now and scribbling notes about algebra was not going to help.

Maths finished and after packing up his things, he left the class and set off down the corridor to the science block. The corridors were narrow and avoiding bumping into other students was a hard task in itself. The noise of students talking to each other about what they had been up to at the weekend filled the space and just from walking from maths to science he had caught up on all the recent gossip that was going around. Kacy Grange and Gary Stead had broken up for the fifteenth time, Barry Winks had gotten drunk at Henrietta Winslow's party at the weekend and threw up in her mum's wardrobe and the juiciest information of all was that Mr. Ebbs and Miss Reah from the Science Department had been seen out together over the weekend - and they were holding hands! Arnold was quite happy keeping himself to himself at school and didn't feel he needed a large circle of friends. He was quite happy with the ones he had or should that be the ONE he had. He continued to make his way up the crowded corridor but soon began to feel like a sardine crammed into a tin, so he made for the exit and decided to walk across the courtyard as it was much less crowded and quieter.

Arnold was normally good at the rest of the morning's subjects though he always did the bare minimum that he could get away with, as he did not find them interesting. His favourite subject was History which he had later that day. He always fully participated in this subject which was easy because he had a great teacher in Mr. Higgins, a man who worked tirelessly to keep the class engaged. Arnold was enjoying these lessons even more now as they were studying the history around spirit beasts. He felt as though he might learn something that would help him in encouraging his own spirit beast to manifest and for this reason, he was especially looking forward to it.

After what felt like the longest of eternities, Arnold had made it through two horrifically boring lessons, and it was finally lunchtime. He had made his way into the dining hall and found himself a seat at one of the benches and started to make his way through the ham and cheese sandwiches that his mum had made for him. He was still trying to come to conclusions about his dream, so much so that the noisy hustle and bustle of dinner time felt like white noise in the background; he was aware of it but didn't pay any attention to it. Otto joined him at the table, sitting opposite him with a daft grin on his face. He was looking across at Arnold as if he was waiting to be prompted about what he was thinking. Arnold looked back at him across the dinner table which looked as though it was about a hundred years old and covered in the scribes of many of the students that had attended the school before him. He did not say a word but waited for his friend to speak.

"Maybe you are a bat!" he blurted out excitedly, unable to contain his theory any longer. It appeared Arnold wasn't the only one who had spent the morning contemplating what his dreams could be a sign of. Arnold had just taken a huge gulp of his orange juice and he had to stop himself spitting it out across the table in front of him as he forced laughter back down. He took a moment to gather himself.

"I don't think so, Otto. The way I am flying in my dreams is as though I'm gliding. The way bats fly is scatty and erratic - it wouldn't make sense to be a bat." He let out a sigh as he finished his sandwich before helping it down with another big gulp of juice. "I just wish that my spirit beast would give me some sort of sign and not just in a dream. I mean why can't anything be happening to me like it is for you?". Feeling a wave of frustration come over him, Arnold couldn't help but feel guilty as the irritation he was showing must seem to Otto as though he was mad at him. He needed to get a grip on his feelings and not let his frustrations consume him.

Out of nowhere, a loud crash could be heard from across the hall. It sounded as though a metal tray had been dropped and Arnold waited for the usual sarcastic cheer to echo through the dining hall. However, this did not happen, and he looked across to the other side of the hall to where there appeared to be some sort of commotion. He could hear the whispers from the other children who were forming a large circle around something, their whispers slowly turning into chanting. Arnold stood there expecting a fight to have broken out but again he was wrong. The younger children had started to run away from the circle that had formed whilst the older kids moved towards the disturbance. Otto and Arnold exchanged a look at each other before nodding in silent, almost telepathic, agreement and ran across the hall, pushing their way through the large crowd to see what all the fuss was about. With surprising ease, they found themselves at the front only to find themselves stood with their mouths open wide, unable to believe what they were seeing.

"Bloody hell," Otto whispered.

Stood there with a look of confusion, bewilderment and excitement was Everett Harris. Everett was an intelligent girl from

Arnold's History class. She was pretty but known for her short temper which made her intimidating to most of the boys in their class. Otto had often joked to him that her spirit beast would be a bull due to her 'bull in a china shop' attitude. Otto had apparently got this wrong, as stood there - in front of Everett - was her spirit beast, which had manifested for the first time and completely out of the blue, judging by the panicked expression on Everett's face. Her eyes were an iced blue colour which looked intense against her dark skin, her gaze fixed firmly in front of her.

"Well, that's a little embarrassing," Otto mumbled, "At least I was kind of right." Arnold couldn't help but laugh as he stared across in awe at the spirit beast that was stood in front of them all. A soft blue glow emitted from a small boar that was stood on the table, knocking everything on it flying, as it kicked out also in a panicked state. He could tell it was a boar by the two small tusks protruding from its mouth, underneath its large, round snout. The boar was sniffing loudly, nuzzling its snout on the table clearly over sensitised by the different smells emitting from the food in the dining hall. Arnold could not believe his eyes. He had never seen a spirit beast so up close before and he stood there, analysing every part of it and wanting to absorb as much information as he could before the boar vanished again.

"It's rude to stare," Everett snapped at the group that had formed, her cheeks red with the embarrassment at what was happening. Arnold couldn't help but feel sorry for her, given the current situation. This was the first time Everett had summoned her spirit beast and she had done it by accident, unexpectedly and in front of everyone in the dining hall. The boar shook its body starting from its head and moving all the way down to its short tail, as though it was readying itself for something and then it started to pad its feet on the floor.

"It's going to charge!" a voice called out from the crowd.

As predicted, the spirit beast ran full pelt down the table, knocking all the lunches that were on it into the air, off the table, spilling everything all over the floor. There was a combination of screams and nervous laughter from the other students as the boar hurtled down the hall to the other side, running underneath the tables, bumping into the legs and causing the remaining lunches to also come crashing to the ground.

"I don't know what to do! What do I do now?" Everett panicked, hoping someone in the hall would help.

"How do you expect us to know?" laughed Otto. "Clearly, we are lacking in the, ahem, spirit beast department. Why not try stopping it trashing the hall first, eh? Might be a good start - need a hand?"

Everett nodded with a look of desperation and the boys knew they couldn't let her do this on her own. The poor girl looked absolutely mortified at the whole situation. They needed to help her as it was the right thing to do; after all, this could have happened to any of them and Arnold liked to think that someone would help if he was stood in Everett's shoes. It wasn't uncommon for people's first time to happen in front of others and the last thing Arnold would want would be for loads of people to be stood gawping at him.

Everett and Otto set off chasing the boar around the hall, trying their hardest to catch it. They only managed to antagonise her spirit beast further as it continued to kick out and shake its head around aggressively. It charged at Otto, seemingly unimpressed at his attempts to stop it, clattering straight into his legs and sending him crashing over a table. A loud thud could be heard followed by a yelp as he hit the floor and a tray of food landed on top of him, the other students still stood around watching laughing at his misfortune, much to his annoyance. His cheeks reddened at the embarrassment caused.

"You need to settle it Everett!" Arnold shouted across the hall. He knew a lot about spirit beasts as he was fascinated by them and had done lots of reading around them. It had become a bit of an obsession. "You need to calm and reassure it; it's just as panicked as you are." Arnold found himself offering this advice as he was sure that he had read it in one of the many books he owned on spirit beasts. "Remember it is connected to you, to your emotions." He ran back across the hall to help Otto back to his feet, pulling him up and brushing away the sandwich fillings that were on his blazer.

Everett looked back across the dining hall at them both, unsure what to do but began to try and gather herself before shrugging her shoulders and walking steadily towards her spirit beast which had backed itself into a corner. Slowly, Everett made her way towards the spectral boar and placed her hand out towards it. Although her hand was shaking, she was able to place it on the back of her spirit beast. With this contact, the boar appeared to calm. It turned its head and nuzzled into Everett's hand, making a soft grunting noise. A rare smile came across Everett's face and Arnold could not help but think how pretty she looked as her spirit beast began to dissipate and absorb back into her.

"I can't believe it!" Arnold was so happy to see a spirit beast so up close. Otto had the same blank face that Arnold had. "Tell me about it!" He paused for a second before continuing, "Everett smiled."

At this point, the large double doors to the dining hall swung open and Miss Elstone walked in having been summoned to the hall by the dinner ladies who had witnessed the commotion. She stood there aghast at the state of the hall. She was a short woman and had a plump frame, her long grey hair was tied back into a bun which sat on the top of her head. She had her hands placed firmly on her hips, her bright orange cardigan distracting Arnold from the frustration etched across her face.

"Everybody out!" she bellowed, and just like she had cast a spell, everyone began to leave. "Except you three." She gestured across the hall at Everett, Otto and Arnold and the three stood still in their tracks. "You three will spend the rest of the day cleaning this mess up."

"But we-" Otto began, but he was quickly shot down by Miss Elstone who simply raised her hand to gesture for him to shut up.

"Miss Harris, you are not the first to have the misfortune of this happening in a public place and you will not be the last. However, there is a mess in the hall that needs cleaning and as it was your spirit beast, I am afraid you will have to take responsibility." Her tone was serious and her face stony and rigid. She was clearly unimpressed with the mess. "Master Ethon, Master Redburn as I have been informed you seemed so eager to chase her spirit beast around the hall, you can also help."

Arnold felt hard done by Miss Elstone; after all, they were only trying to help Everett. However, there was no winning Miss Elstone over. The deputy headteacher was renowned as a strict disciplinarian who most found intimidating and did not dare cross. The three of them knew that they would not get anywhere with protesting what had been asked of them so they set off cleaning the large dining hall, which suddenly seemed even bigger with just the three of them in it. The plate-glass windows that had not been replaced since the 70s filled the perimeter ensuring that just enough natural light filled the hall without the need to switch the lights on. The clanging of trays echoed from Otto making a point that he was not happy at being forced to clean them up and Arnold stood with a mop, cleaning the floor with a combination of cheap bleach and other cleaning products which gave the mixture a slightly overpowering lemon smell. There was so much debris on the floor that he needed to change the water several times as he made his way across the room.

"This is torture Arnold, worse than prison," complained Otto, carrying more trays than he could clearly manage. He walked across to the kitchen door to take them in and wash them, mumbling to himself. Once through the door, there was a loud clatter as Otto inevitably dropped the trays. Everett and Arnold set about laughing. The two of them had got a good system. Everett would sweep the food into piles on the floor and using a dustpan and brush, put it in the bin before Arnold would then mop up behind her. Looking at what they had managed to do he felt that they should be done before their final period was finishing, meaning they shouldn't be getting any detentions. Not today, anyway.

"I just want to say thank you for helping me," Everett said, putting her brush to one side and stopping for a short rest. "Everyone else was too busy staring and laughing at me. I appreciate the help."

"Wow, a thank you. Not like you, Everett," Otto called from beyond the hatch.

"Funny. Forget what I said then," she snapped back.

"Ignore him," said Arnold, his cheeks immediately starting to give off a soft glow at her nod of appreciation at his support. He quickly turned away so that Everett didn't notice but not fast enough to make sure Otto didn't. There was a small silence and then Arnold blurted out "What did it feel like?"

"Erm, embarrassing," Everett answered, taken aback at Arnold's sudden question. She let down her brown hair to re-tie it with a bobble before setting off sweeping the floor again.

"Not the situation...how did it feel summoning your spirit beast? What was it like?" He continued to shuffle along the floor mopping away the trail of destruction that had been left by the very spirit beast he was asking about.

"Really strange if I'm honest." She stopped brushing again to answer his question. "I had a strange sensation in my stomach, a sickly kind of feeling. I remember feeling annoyed that some boy had just jumped in the chair I was about to sit on and before I knew it, it was stood there, and I was freaking out. I can't believe that out of all the spirit beasts I have a boar."

"A boar is pretty cool if you ask me," Arnold said. Everett frowned.

"Really? I haven't got a clue what it means, I will have to speak to my dad when I get home to find out more about it."

Arnold knew a lot about her spirit beast as he had read a lot of books on them in his quest to figure out what his own spirit beast would be. "Pig like spirit beasts are deemed to be some of the most intelligent which most people don't realise. The boar is thought to be wilder than pigs but are renowned for their courage as well as their overall fierceness," he explained, practically word for word from the last book he read on the subject. "At least I think that's what it is and if it is, I think that it compliments you really well."

"Thanks." There was a short pause from Everett. "I guess," she said, not really knowing how to take Arnold's comments. Stepping in on his friend's behalf, Otto jumped into the conversation.

"It's Arnold's birthday at the weekend. Fancy coming to the cinema with us?"

"Otto!" He could have killed him, diving in like that. Arnold could feel his face beginning to get warm as his cheeks grew red again.

"Sure, why not? I've nothing else planned. Don't be getting any ideas though, boys."

Otto gave Arnold a cheeky wink. "You can thank me later," he mouthed, silently. Arnold didn't think it was that obvious that he fancied Everett but if Otto had realised it, it must be. The three of them spent the remainder of the school day cleaning and managed to get it done before the day was out. A new friendship had begun to develop, and Arnold couldn't help but feel his circle of friends had just got a little bit bigger. Today was a good day.

Chapter Three

Sat in a chair in a quaint little flat, a man sat drinking a cup of tea out of an old bone china teacup, gazing out of the window to watch the world go by. He could see part of his reflection through the window; he wasn't the strapping young man he used to be. He had a weary face, one that looked as though the owner had experienced a lot of pain in his life. The wrinkles on his forehead resembled the lines of an athletics track, running from one side to the other. He had always blamed his busy work life from years past and the stresses that came with it for his deeply furrowed brow.

The sound of two clocks ticking in the background could be heard though not in tandem with each other, which would drive most people quite mad. The old boy had become used to the noise, to the point where he hardly noticed the ticking noise at all. Placing his teacup down on the table, it made a soft clinking noise as he picked up the teapot and filled his cup once more. He brought it to his mouth and slurped his tea, letting out a small sigh of appreciation. He did like a nice pot of tea.

The small flat felt cluttered with personal treasures and mementos from his eventful life and career filling the glass cabinet and every inch of spare surface in the room, from on top of the fire to sections of the dining table. On the walls, there were pictures of a younger version of himself with friends from years ago, on different expeditions that had taken him all over the world.

Stood next to him in one photo was a beautiful red-haired lady with enchanting green eyes, the colour resembling that of a sparkling emerald just as the light had caught them. The photos on the wall eventually became ones of this enchantingly beautiful woman and himself on various dates   - from bowling to the outdoor cinema - before ending with photos of their wedding day. He sighed. What a magical day that had been!

He often thought fondly of the moments that he had shared with his wife. Looking back brought him much happiness and was tinged with only a few regrets which is why there were so many photographs scattered around the room in mismatched frames; his personal museum of an extraordinary life.

Despite the happy memories, he sometimes felt an emptiness inside which started two years ago by the unbearable grief of his wife's death. She was the person with whom he had shared everything and when she had left him, he felt a sense of bitterness towards fate. At the time of his wife's passing, he had desperately wished it had been he that had been taken by the pneumonia that plagued her in her later years and then cruelly stole her life.

She balanced out his personality and had brought out a better side to him; without her, he was now a lonely, bitter man who had quickly become a recluse. He was uninterested in most things and he simply didn't care for a world without his beloved wife. After a marriage that had spanned 40 years, the fact of the matter was that he simply did not know what to do without her. He had very few friends, a result of his social isolation and the icy touch of death catching up with them all in their old age. So, without his soulmate, life just felt like an unending, lonely struggle.

Noticing the time on the small, old fashioned, gold clock that stood at the centre of the table where he sat drinking his tea, he realised it was time to head towards town to complete the day's tasks. These consisted of collecting some items from the supermarket for his evening meal and maybe go to the local bookies to place a couple of pounds worth of bets on the football that would be on later that afternoon. Short trips into town were about the most adventurous he got nowadays, opting to spend most of his time either reading or watching television in the comfort of his home. Since his wife's passing, he had found that he no longer had much tolerance for other people and hated the pointless fake conversations that society insisted upon, whenever he left the house. He had no time for this. He would much rather go into town, do what he needed to do and return to the comforts of his flat where no one would bother him.

He watched from his window as two local football teams played on the field adjacent to his flat. The grass was, for the most part, in good condition, apart from where the goalkeepers stood. This area of the pitch had become extremely muddy and the keepers were filthy in comparison to their teammates due to flailing around in the mud, like ecstatic pigs. His window was slightly open to allow the air to circulate in his room and he could hear the players shouting to each other. He could also hear one of the managers who was screaming instructions at one of the players, clearly unimpressed by his performance. The man smiled to himself, thinking back to when he was younger; he used to be quite the footballer himself. He had held the position of left-back and been involved in many league titles. Those were the times! Now here he was in his later years, struggling to simply climb the stairs leading up to his flat. This greatly frustrated him. His age wasn't just catching up with him, it had overtaken him, making most simple tasks an arduous experience for him to endure.

Watching the final minutes of the game, he finished off his cup of tea before putting on his shoes, coat and flat cap and gingerly walked down the steps of his small flat to the front door. He found he had to slightly lean towards the wall to keep his balance, the handrail wobbling as he used it to bear his weight. He hated these stairs and the difficulties they created for him, but he did not want to move and leave all the memories behind. He was also too proud, or stubborn as his wife would have called it, to ask for help by way of having a stairlift put in. To say he was stubborn at times was putting it mildly though to him, he was simply too proud to ask for help. Locking his front door and hobbling down the cobbled path of his garden, he looked at his small maintained garden with varying flowers and bushes before turning and heading down the road towards his local supermarket. Maybe he would treat himself to a bottle of his favourite red wine to have this evening; it was Saturday after all, he thought to himself. The weather report had forecast intermittent showers throughout the day and for this reason, he did not want to be out too long. The weather was looking slightly overcast with the sun trying to burn its way through the greying clouds.

Making it to the supermarket, he slowly wandered around the maze-like aisles, collecting the items he needed for tea. The floor looked like it had been buffed to within an inch of its existence, creating a shine on the floor that he had only ever seen at a bowling alley. He couldn't help but wonder how people his age were expected to walk on the highly polished surface without slipping. He edged around the ever increasingly dangerous environment with even more care, this latest obstacle joining the long lists of hazards he now faced daily.

When he had finished collecting his items, he made his way to the checkout area using a small trolley he had acquired to keep himself balanced. The young checkout assistant scanned his items and gave him a smile that he didn't respond to and he packed the items into the bag for life he had brought with him to save him having to buy yet another plastic carrier bag. He left the supermarket with his stress levels slightly above what they were when he had first entered.

Next, he headed across to his local bookmakers to place a bet on the afternoon's football. He opted for three different variations of a fivefold accumulator for this afternoon's matches. He was feeling lucky today and he enjoyed watching the scores as they unfolded over the weekend, even though he very rarely won on his accumulators. Managing to avoid most conversation and having to only engage with the bookie to place his bet, he left the bookmakers. Looking up at the sky, he decided he should head back to his flat, as the clouds had darkened, and it looked as though the heavens were about to open. He briefly contemplated going back into the bookmakers and asking for them to ring a taxi for him, but he decided against this as he didn't want to waste money when he lived so close. A little down the road he regretted that decision, as shortly after setting off the weather turned, and it started to rain heavily. Even he couldn't help but regret his stubbornness on this occasion.

The clouds darkened, the rain bouncing from the pavement. The sudden change in the weather surprised him as only a light shower had been forecast. Soon the rain turned into an unforgiving storm, the water stinging as it lashed his strained face and the wind pushing against him every step of the way. Within moments he was drenched to the bone; he may as well have jumped in a swimming pool for how wet he was. Stopping for a moment, he assessed which route may be the best to get back to the warmth of his home where he could dry off and put his feet up for the rest of the day. He squinted his eyes to reduce the amount of rain hitting them whilst looking across the increasingly flooded football field to his house on the opposite side.

A pathway down the side of the field led the way home though normally he would walk all the way around, avoiding this route due to the local youths who tended to congregate and intimidate anyone trying to pass. The rain was now coming down even heavier and unable to see anyone standing around on this route, he decided he would take the narrow footpath by the side of the field. Trudging down along the path, he attempted to avoid the puddles that had quickly formed as he didn't feel like spoiling his new suede shoes that were a recent purchase. Deep down he already knew that they had been damaged by the torrential downpour that he was currently experiencing. Why had he bothered coming out? If the weather report had been accurate and he had known the weather would be like this, he would have jumped in a taxi and he was cursing the fact that he hadn't.

"Charles Grey!" The deep voice boomed aggressively from behind him. The voice did not say his name like you would if you thought you recognised somebody. This voice sounded like he knew exactly who Charles was and somehow, he knew this wasn't a good thing. Stopping in his tracks, Charles felt a shudder down his spine and a sudden spike in his adrenaline. His heart began to race. He could not decide whether he recognised the voice of the man who had just called his name but what he did know was the sense of dread that came over him as he turned around.

Turning slowly to see who had just bellowed his name, the rain made it difficult for his already deteriorating eyesight to make out any details of the man he might recognise. Stood in front of him was a tall, powerfully built man wearing a long black overcoat, the rain cascading down his jacket and his fists tightly clenched. He could just about make out his face and he did not recognise it. There were three, cracked scars down one side of his face symmetrical with each other making him look even more sinister. The man smiled before beginning to speak again.

"Charles Grey," He bellowed once more. "I have been looking for you for some time. It has taken a while but here you are...I can sense you; I can sense it. You have been here all along." The scarred stranger was furious at him, the aggression in his voice was very telling and equally as frightening.

Charles stepped back startled; this man knew who he was, what he used to do. How could this be though? He had kept himself to himself since retiring and there were only a handful of people around that knew him personally and professionally. Charles had happily lived a quiet life in his later years to keep himself and his late wife, safe.

"I-I have no-no idea what you mean." The words stuttered out of his mouth with little confidence whilst stepping backwards away from the stranger.

"Please don't take me for a fool, I know exactly who you are," He sneered, a twisted smile on his face. He pulled his jacket to the side and revealed the hilt of his blade. It was jet black, with intricate carvings decorating the side of it. He took hold of the hilt and began to unsheathe the weapon, showing the bone white that he was now wielding. Charles recoiled in horror at what he was seeing and for a moment he froze. He recognised the blade and instantaneously understood what he was there to do. His heart sank, his mouth instantly becoming dry and his entire body began to tremble. He was too old, too frail to try and outrun the man and he was unarmed. He began to survey his surroundings, thinking of what to do next and trying to come up with some sort of plan. He gripped his shopping bag tightly, realising there was no easy way out of this situation. He would certainly put up a fight if he had to; he was unsure he would still have it in him but was willing to give it a try.

Before he knew it, the attacker ran at him with great speed, swinging the blade back and aiming a strike at Charles, the black blade glistening unnaturally in the rain. Charles swung the bag he was carrying and slammed it into the side of his attacker's head as he lunged toward him. Diving out of the way of the blade he rolled to try and gain some distance between himself and his attacker, showing the agility of someone in prime fitness and not that of an elderly man.

"I knew it was you," the stranger breathed, his crooked smile contorting his scarred face as his lip bled from the blow. He ran at Charles again, this time aiming a kick which made contact with his target as he lay on the floor. The blow sent Charles rolling over on his side, through the mud of the field and came to a stop in a large puddle that had formed by the path.

Gasping for his breath and heavily winded by the strike, he attempted to pick himself up from the floor, his hands gripping the heavy mud that had formed beneath him. Charles attempted to pick himself up, but his arms buckled, and he fell back to the floor, rolling onto his back. He lay there, his chest convulsing as he attempted to regain breath and his clothes sticking to him tightly as he became covered in the rain and mud. He felt utterly alone. No one was around to help him and at that moment he couldn't help but wonder if anyone would notice when he was gone. An intense feeling of sadness overcame as he lay there, knowing that this was it and that his time was up though he was able to take comfort in the knowledge that he would soon be reunited with his wife.

Within seconds of thinking of his wife, he had a feeling in the pit of his stomach, one he had not experienced for a very long time. His body began to start to emit a soft yellow glow and suddenly a warm sensation came over him, his breathing steadied itself and his chest no longer throbbed where he had been struck. He felt calmer knowing he did not have time to dwell on the situation. He began to climb to his knees as if being guided by strings that were pulling him to his feet. Something wanted him to get up and fight back. Managing to get to one knee he planted his other foot firmly on the muddy floor, ready to stand up and prepare himself should the man strike him again.

He felt rejuvenated like he was in his prime again and it was a good feeling; a feeling that had been a long time coming. It was as though a deep fog that was in his mind had instantaneously cleared and the path he needed to walk was now obvious.

The rain continued to pour down on the two of them. The scarred man stalked over to Charles, swinging the blade he was carrying downwards towards him with incredible force. Looking up at him and knowing he was not done for yet, Charles raised his hands above his head and grabbed the hilt of the blade as well as his attacker's hands before pushing him away with equal force, as though he had turned his attacker's strength against him. Realisation drifted across his face; he recognised that blade. It was extremely dangerous, especially if this stranger knew what it was capable of. This blade was an ancient artefact.

The man steadied himself from being pushed backwards and grinned at Charles again. His mouth was thin, and he was now looking even more sinister than before. He was not surprised at the strength shown by Charles, this fraud of a frail old man, though it had still annoyed him that he had been able to push him back. He set off at speed again towards Charles raising his blade above him.

"That's a good start, Charles. Now show me it. I want to see it!" he seethed, the anger in his voice rising adjacent to his impatience. The scarred man was becoming increasingly more annoyed at Charles' reluctance to show him what he wanted to see.

Charles, however, was feeling energised. The kick he had received earlier was a distant memory even though he thought the pain in his side was an indication that when all this was done and his auro faded, he would feel the pain again of the broken rib he had received from the initial blow.

He knew he had no option but to cave to the scarred man's demands if he was to survive this night. He just desperately hoped that he still had his lifelong companion within him after all this time. Raising his hands in the air he began to move them around in a motion not too dissimilar to a figure of eight, the motion smooth, almost rhythmic. He continued with this motion, the yellow glow from his auro leaving a light trail behind his hands, allowing the shape he was forming to light up the air around him. His auro increased around him whilst he continued, his hands moving faster and faster. Charles began to feel the sensation of something rising within him. He had forgotten how this felt and held back a wave of nausea that overcame him to continue with what he was doing.

The attacker remained still, his horrifically disfigured face lit up from the yellow glow that Charles was emitting, intrigued by what he was seeing and excited by what was about to happen. He tightened the grip on his blade, biding his time before his next move, the rain still pouring down his heavily scarred face. He had waited a long time and travelled a long way for this moment and he just hoped that the old man was as powerful as he anticipated.

A bright flash of light lit up the field in front of Charles as his spirit beast began to form. Charles continued the motion with his hands in the air and concentrated on his beast taking its form. He had not done this for several years and hoped that he would not fail, knowing full well that if he did, his time would be up. Letting out a roar of anger and frustration at the attacker, Charles finished motioning his hands, the roar of his voice overtaken by the deafening roar of his spirit beast, which was now stood in front of him in its powerful form of a hippo. The spectral hippo looked battle-worn; its thick grey skin cracked with the many skirmishes it had experienced in the past. The rain cascading down its body made its skin look shiny, reflecting the light from Charles auro. A glow of light emitted from around it which matched its anchor and it stood there, staring down the scarred man, ready to defend Charles.

The attacker began laughing to himself and began to wave his blade about playfully in a circular motion, a demonstration of how easy he could wield his blade. The spirit beast glanced at Charles and let out a soft rumble as if it was asking whether Charles was ok. Charles nodded back at the hippo which turned to face the attacker again before letting out another deafening roar. This alone nearly knocked the scarred man back, the sheer noise from the roar hitting him in the heart and startling him. He knew it would be powerful but expected nothing of this magnitude. They began to run at one another, the hippo bearing its large protruding teeth and the scarred man with his blade outstretched. The hippo smashed its head into him, sending him hurtling backwards through the field. He was quickly back to his feet, however, but the spirit beast was upon him with its large gaping mouth wide open, attempting to bite him. The scarred man jumped back, narrowly missing the hippo's attack before regaining his balance. This was exactly what he had been waiting for and he was enjoying being in this moment, testing the old man's power.

The hippo attempted to bite again, only this time the man grabbed hold of the spirit beast's jaws, stopping it from chomping down on him. Charles could not believe the strength his attacker was displaying; he should not have been able to hold his spirit beast's jaws like he was doing.

"You know how to wield that blade," he called across to the scarred man, realising what he would be able to do to his spirit beast. The man continued to struggle with the beast before pushing its head backwards, his hands slipping in the process due to the rain, He managed to dive to the side avoiding the enormous creature's powerful jaws as they came crashing down. The hippo quickly and instinctively swung its large paddle-like tail out from the side, catching the scarred man in the ribs and sending him crashing to the ground again. The scarred man got back to his feet spitting some blood onto the floor, his twisted smile returning to his snarling face. Breathing heavily, they readied themselves to run at each other again. The rain was bouncing heavily around them as they both stood their ground, the man staring into the eyes of the spirit beast that stood before him. He was unfazed by the power shown by the hippo and he ran at the glowing spirit beast, blade outstretched, ready to finish what he had started. He knew what he needed to do, and nothing was going to stop him from achieving his goal. The waiting was over, and he was about to seal the old man's fate.

Chapter Four

Arnold was flying. The feeling of being so high up and without a care in the world really was amazing. He just felt so free. He was not as high up as usual but again he could feel the icy, tingling sensation of the wind against his brown, tan wings. It was truly sensational and like nothing he had experienced. Catching a gust of wind, he flew up higher, riding the wind and taking the opportunity to absorb the view. And what a view it was! The sky was bright blue, only punctuated by an occasional white cloud. The wind was calm which made it easy to glide through the air with minimum effort. In the distance, he saw snow-covered mountains like a cake that had been dusted with icing from above, the snow clean and untouched. At the base of the mountains, there were pine trees, protruding from the ground, also with a slight dusting of snow over them. Then he saw the calming waters of a lake, the water so bright and blue that if not for the mountains it would be hard to differentiate it from the sky above.

Swooping down from the sky he flew level with the lake, his feet touching the very surface of the water with enough tenderness to leave a slight jet stream behind him. The icy chill of the water on his feet felt quite refreshing. Catching another gust of wind, he swept high up into the sky again so he could see the vast fields and hills of the countryside beneath him. The buzz he experienced when gliding through the air was so exhilarating. Arnold had never experienced anything like this before and he didn't want it to end. Arnold gasped to himself, awestruck at the landscape that appeared to be infinite, wondering how far the land could go on for. He reached the brow of another large hill and was instantaneously drawn to something in his periphery vision that had become visible in the sweeping landscape. A building or a tower of some description sat at the top of one of the hills in the distance, too far away to clearly make out any details. Intrigued by what he could see he set off towards the building to investigate, curious as to what it might be.

Arnold's heart raced as he was awoken by the loud shrieking noise going off right next to his head, the noise shrill and piercing his ears with such force he could already feel the beginnings of a headache. The noise was coming from the small clock by the side of his bed and Arnold wondered to himself how such a small thing could create so much noise. He couldn't help feeling annoyed with himself for two reasons; not only had his alarm woke him up from his dream, but it was also a Saturday and he had forgotten to turn the stupid thing off. Arnold reached out in a daze, the uncoordinated motion knocking the clock off his bedside drawers and sending it crashing to the floor, creating even more noise. He must have woken everybody up with that. Arnold was now lying in bed completely wide awake at seven o'clock on a Saturday morning, all because he had forgotten to unplug the alarm. Trying to return to his dream, he attempted to get back to sleep so that he could jump back in where he left off but after an hour of tossing and turning, he decided he might as well get up. He sat up in bed, stretched and let out a large yawn before stepping into his slippers and making his way downstairs.

As he turned the corner from the foot of the stairs to the front room, he was greeted by a large banner which read HAPPY BIRTHDAY! in large multi-coloured letters. "Happy birthday, sweetheart!" His mum came sweeping out of the kitchen and gave Arnold a suffocating hug. His dad walked in behind him, ruffling his already bed-worn hair and wished him a happy birthday too. "Fifteen? How on earth did that sneak up on us?" he laughed. "Seems like only two minutes ago we were bringing you back from the hospital".

"Thanks, Mum, thanks, Dad." Struggling to breathe within his mum's grasp, he shook his head and attempted to peel her arms from around him. He had been looking forward to his birthday, not for the gifts but for the fact that he was now at the prime age for his spirit beast to manifest itself. He knew it was only a matter of time but could not help feeling frustrated that nothing had physically happened to him yet. He would happily trade all his birthday presents just to know what his spirit beast would be or to even get a physical sign.

Arnold spent the morning making his way through the pile of cards he had received before starting to unwrap his birthday presents. Arnold's favourite present was the first-person role-playing game that his mum and dad had bought for him. No sooner had Arnold finished unwrapping his presents and got himself dressed than there was a sudden knock at the door. He instantly knew who was stood behind the door as he recognised it as the same knock he heard every morning before school. Walking to the front door, he grasped the handle and opened it to reveal Otto standing there, with a beaming smile on his face. It was the kind of face you would see on a three-year-old who had walked into a room filled with presents after Father Christmas had been.

"Well?" he asked. "Did you get it?" He was looking at Arnold with his eyes wide open like he had had one too many cans of energy drink and would burst if Arnold didn't put him out of his misery soon.

Arnold laughed out loud at how he looked, standing in the doorway.

"Happy Birthday, Arnold, oh thanks Otto, do come in," his sarcastic tone going straight over Otto's head. Otto looked slightly confused. He was truly terrible at reading people and understanding sarcasm was too much of an ask; he just didn't get it. Arnold stepped to the side to allow his friend to enter and smiled. "I got it." The two ran upstairs so they could test the game out and they continued testing it for the next couple of hours.

"I had another dream last night." Arnold had begun to tell Otto about his most recent dream. "At the time it feels so real but when I wake up, the more I try to remember it, the more distant it seems to become." Otto sat crossed legged on the beanbag in the middle of Arnold's bedroom, engrossed in the new game that they were playing.

"I spoke to my dad last night when I got home and he told me to tell you," Otto said, pausing as he concentrated on shooting someone in the game they were playing online. "Get in, did you see that?" he said, celebrating his win with a fist pump. He looked over at Arnold, proud of his manoeuvre that took out the opposition on the game with a sublime headshot. Arnold stared at Otto in disbelief at his ridiculously short attention span. "What?"

Arnold let out a loud sigh. "Your dad told you to tell me what?"

"Sorry, he told me to tell you, well, apparently your dreams are most vivid when you first wake up and the longer you leave it after waking up, the less you will remember." Otto stuffed one of Arnold's mint chocolate truffles that he got from his aunt and uncle for his birthday in his mouth before he continued.

"And?" Arnold prompted.

"Basically, you need to keep a pad next to your bed and as soon as you wake up, jot down the details and better still draw anything specific that you see." Otto smirked at Arnold, proud that for once he had contributed something productive to their conversation. This didn't happen often for Otto and he liked to savour these moments. Arnold rummaged through one of his drawers until he found the pad he was looking for and placed this on his bedside drawers next to his alarm clock.

"I wonder if Everett had any dreams before her spirit beast manifested?" He sat on his bed and sighed loudly, putting one of his chocolates in his mouth.

"Think you should just ask her mate." Otto had a knack for stating the obvious.

"Maybe I will when we see her later."

"You'll bottle it."

"Whatever." Arnold felt a wave of jealousy come across him. It wasn't fair that Otto and all the others in his year at school were either showing signs of their spirit beast or were already able to summon one. But no. All he was left with were dreams of flying and what use was that to anyone? Arnold didn't care what his spirit beast was, he just wanted something more than a dumb dream to happen to him. Arnold picked his controller thinking that maybe shooting some people on his game might distract him for a short while. He slouched into the beanbag that Otto had vacated in the middle of the room and set up another match. Otto picked up the other controller and the two began frantically bashing buttons as soon as it loaded.

Sometime later, there was another knock at the door. Arnold knew who it was as he had been waiting all morning for him to get there. Arnold ran down the stairs two at a time and flung the front door open to reveal Arnold's Grandad, stood there dressed in his usual green jacket, hat, and striped blue and white scarf. Arnold adored his Grandad and loved spending time with him. He would often call round after school to have tea with him and the two were incredibly close; to Arnold, his Grandad was the most important person in the world.

"Happy birthday, Arnold!" He opened his arms in a manner to welcome Arnold in for an embrace. He stepped forward and gave his Grandad a warm hug.

"Thanks, Grandad" he replied as he stepped back to make room for him to come in. Stepping into the house, he took off his hat and removed his coat. He always dressed smartly and today was no exception; he had opted for a yellow shirt and a pale blue tie. He wore a green jumper over the top, but the shirt and tie could still be seen due to the v neck style of his jumper. He still had a full head of white hair which was slicked back, albeit slightly matted from wearing his cap. His eyes looked tired, yet still sparkled at the sight of his grandson.

Arnold, Otto, who had followed Arnold down the stairs, and his Grandad walked through into the living room where his Grandad passed him an envelope. Arnold opened it to find a birthday card with a picture of a monkey on it. He also found twenty pounds had been put inside.

"Thanks, Grandad" Arnold felt grateful for the money his Grandad had put inside his card.

Arnold's grandad sat down in his favourite chair. It creaked almost as loudly as he groaned as he got himself comfortable.

"I'm sorry it's only money this year Arnold but I really struggled with what to get you." He leaned over and gestured for a cup of tea. Arnold left the room before returning a few minutes later with a fresh brew.

"Maybe you could get yourself some aftershave to impress the girls at school. I was courting when I was your age." His grandad chuckled to himself. Arnold felt a rush of blood to his cheeks and knew instantly that he had started blushing. He hated blushing due to the fact it drew attention to him and it did not help that he would blush at the slightest thing, something he found really embarrassing. Arnold walked over to the fireplace and placed his card with the others that he had already opened.

"Do you think your spirit beast could be a monkey like on that card, Arnold?" Otto smiled. Arnold shook his head.

"Last I knew, monkeys didn't fly." He replied whilst rolling his eyes. "Not unless you are referring to a certain type of flying monkey last seen on the Wizard of Oz and oh, they are not real". Arnold really was not in the mood to be wound up about his spirit beast, even if it was his birthday.

Otto looked back at Arnold and shrugged his shoulders as he had nothing to come back at him with.

"What do you think my spirit beast could be, Grandad?" Arnold gazed across at his Grandad hoping he could impart some much-needed wisdom. Instead, his Grandad tutted in disapproval of the conversation which deflated Arnold further. Arnold wished he had not said anything; he knew his Grandad didn't like talking about spirit beasts and kicked himself for bringing it up.

"Don't rush it, Arnold" his Grandad snapped. "Having a spirit beast is not all that it is cracked up to be. It's not all fun and games." Arnold's Grandad took a sip of his tea and placed the cup back down on the table. "Your auro needs time to develop." Arnold understood that each person's auro was what connected them to their spirit beasts. Those that had the best connections were those that had fully mastered how to use their auro. "Now if you just want to talk about spirit beasts then I will leave you boys to it and be on my way." He was clearly not in the mood for that topic of conversation. Arnold understood that he did not like to discuss spirit beasts but did he didn't think his grandad needed to be so grumpy about it. Arnold's mum and dad walked into the room, so Arnold and Otto seized the opportunity to leave the room and go back upstairs to Arnold's bedroom.

"What was that?" Otto looked at Arnold, gobsmacked at how blunt his Grandad had been with him. "You ok, mate?" Arnold attempted to brush it off like he was fine, but his Grandad had really upset him. Arnold knew he never liked to speak about spirit beasts or about his time as a Doyen, so Arnold felt foolish for asking. "Why is he so against them?" Otto pressed. Arnold simply shrugged his shoulders limply, unable to explain as he did not know what the issue was. He had never spoken to his Grandad about it due to getting the same reaction he knew he would get and whenever he approached his Dad about it, he simply told Arnold to leave it alone. So, he did. Usually.

"Come on. We had better head to town otherwise we will end up missing the film," Arnold said, not so subtly attempting to switch the topic of conversation. They grabbed their jackets and said goodbye to Arnold's family before heading out the front door and toward the train station. Arnold was looking forward to taking his mind off his spirit beast issues for a while.

Arnold and Otto made it in time for their train and had been on it for about twenty minutes of their thirty-minute journey. They had managed to get seats that sat adjacent to each other so they both sat slouched, facing each other with their feet up on the seats opposite them. Arnold checked his watch to make sure they were still on time for meeting Everett and George.

"Maybe he has forgotten how to summon his spirit beast and that's why he gets grumpy when anyone talks about them?" Otto was on his umpteenth theory about Arnold's Grandad which had ranged from this one to him losing it somewhere. Arnold felt drained by Otto's persistence in coming up with a theory that fit. "Can we not just talk about something else?" he asked. Arnold still felt frustrated that his Grandad would not speak to him about his spirit beast. The two were so close when it came to everything else. Arnold spoke to his Grandad about things he didn't even speak to his parents about, not even Otto. It really hurt him that he wouldn't even listen to him about his dreams or even advise him about the changes that he would be going through soon.

Arnold couldn't dress it up; he felt let down by his Grandad. However, he picked himself up and forced a smile at Otto, determined not to let it spoil his birthday. After all, he was fifteen and before long, he would have his very own spirit beast.

"Ahem, feet." Arnold and Otto noticed the ticket conductor standing over them. The woman looked fed up, her eyes cutting through them both like daggers. They decided not to push their luck and quickly moved their feet off the seats. The boys looked a little bit sheepish, but luckily for them, the train drew to a halt and they knew they had arrived at their station. The two stood up to leave and moved towards the door avoiding eye contact with the ticket conductor. "Ahem." The ticket conductor's second cough drew their attention to the fact they were facing the wrong way and needed to turn around to exit the train via the opposite doors. The doors couldn't open soon enough for them, mortified at the few sniggers coming from the passengers that were aware of the error they made. Arnold could feel the glow of his blushing cheeks which made him feel even more embarrassed. The doors opened after what felt like an eternity and the two exited and walked down the road, heading for the cinema.

"Don't mess this up with Everett," Otto said, nudging Arnold. "I have got her to come so just try to be less like you and more like me," he teased. Arnold rolled his eyes.

"I couldn't think of anything worse than being more like you, that would be torture. It's the cinema, what's the worst that can happen?"

Chapter Five

When they reached the cinema, they could see Everett stood there with her best friend George. They were stood at the side of the cinema and both had their spirit beasts summoned, messing around. Everett had her boar spirit beast next to her and George's fox spirit beast was teasing the boar. The boar and the fox were chasing after each other but overall the fox was more agile and too quick for the boar. The fox jumped up on a wall near where Everett and George were stood talking. Everett's boar ran to the wall and let out a series of grunts, appearing frustrated at its inability to scale the wall as the fox had done.

"Watch this, guys," Everett said whilst concentrating heavily on her spirit beast. She switched her focus from the boar to the wall, concentrating deeply on what she wanted her spirit beast to do. The fox lay there with its tail hanging down, still teasing the boar. The boar jumped back and shuffled like it was readying itself for something. Gathering pace, the boar ran at the wall and threw itself at it, causing the wall to shake. As the boar staggered backwards, dazed from the blow, the fox lost its balance and fell from the wall. Everett,

Arnold and Otto set about laughing at what they had just seen Everett's spirit beast do. George, however, stood there stony-faced, clearly unimpressed at Everett's actions. She folded her arms and the three of them stopped laughing, bracing themselves for the lecture they were about to receive.

"That is cruel, Everett." George was the sensible one out of the group and was an advocate for spirit beast rights. "That could have really hurt your spirit beast. How could you be so irresponsible? If you misuse your spirit beast there is a chance it will not summon for you. You have only just learned how to summon it so don't let being reckless ruin it for you. You would be the first to moan if you lost it." George was cross and Everett appeared to be sheepish, trying to avoid the conversation.

"Alriiiight," Everett replied, wanting to move the conversation forward. George smiled back at Everett knowing that this was the best she was going to get out of her. Everett and George had been best friends for as long as they could remember, even before George started shortening her name from Georgina due to her complete dislike of the name that her parents had burdened her with. George also had her own quirky fashion sense and did not like to conform to so-called social norms. Today she was wearing a long black and white striped top that came down to just above her knees, her three-quarter length jeans and a pair of Doc Martin boots. As always, she was wearing her trademark beany hat with just a tiny bit of red curly hair poking out from the front and back of it. George wasn't as abrupt or brash as Everett, but she was not afraid to speak out for something she thought was right or felt passionate about.

"You should start up your own campaign for spirit beast rights, George," Otto grinned as he tried to wind her up. She did not appreciate Otto poking fun at her, and this was obvious from her face which looked more than unimpressed.

"Come on, guys! We need to head in otherwise we are going to miss the film". Arnold was trying his hardest to make sure the movie wasn't ruined by the other three winding each other up. "I'll pay for you Everett if you like, Otto will pay for George". Otto looked disapprovingly towards him.

"Fine, I'll pay for George. It's a bit like a double date this, isn't it?". Otto winked at George knowing that she wasn't his biggest fan.

"Don't kid yourselves, boys," Everett laughed.

Arnold felt a rush of blood fill his cheeks and spun away quickly to avoid the others noticing. Otto turned and headed towards the entrance, wanting to get in first so that he could get his bucket of popcorn and a giant Coke. The other three followed Otto and joined the large queue that had formed to buy their favourite cinema treats. After what felt like an age, they had finally got their tickets and snacks and walked down a dark corridor together towards the double doors that were illuminated by a large number three. Arnold stepped forward pushing one of the doors open with his foot before using his body to hold the door open for the others to enter. Arnold did contemplate letting the door swing back at Otto as this was something he would do, but he opted against it on this occasion. Otto loved to play pranks on others, and it would have been sweet revenge to get him back. They walked up the steps and shuffled along in the dark to find their seats. Arnold sat down next to Otto who placed his popcorn on his knee and scooped a large handful ready to shovel into his mouth. Arnold seized his opportunity and nudged Otto's arm, knocking the popcorn in Otto's hand all over him and Everett. George let out a giggle at her amusement.

"You got me," Otto whispered. "I'll give you that one, which now makes it 10-1 to me". Otto was a prankster but had no issues with being pranked himself.

"Shhhhh!" There was an irate man behind them who did not appreciate them talking and laughing. The four of them sunk down into their seats and settled down to watch the movie. The screen lit up and the pre-movie trailers began to play. As Arnold readied himself for the film, he placed his arm on the rest and realised Everett's arm was already resting there. He quickly pulled his arm away awkwardly and noticed Everett give him a sweet smile. She moved her arm over slightly to allow him some space to rest his arm next to hers, which he nervously acknowledged.

After the movie finished, Arnold, Otto, George and Everett exited the building. They squinted as their eyes adjusted to the natural light outside after being in a darkened room for the last two hours.

"Well, that's two hours of our life we will never get back". Everett was less than impressed with what she had just been made to endure. Otto had a look of pure disbelief at what he had just heard.

"What are you on about Everett? That film was amazing!" Otto was sci-fi mad and even though Arnold also thought the movie was poor, there would be no convincing Otto as he loved and appreciated any such film. Arnold thought back to when Otto made him watch a film called Monster in the Closet. It was truly awful however the more cheesy and naff the film was the more Otto would enjoy it. "Come on we need to head back to the train station," Otto said, pointing at his watch. He did not want to miss the train for two reasons; one being that if they missed this train it would be another two hours before the next one and the other was that they could not be late back with Arnold for his birthday tea. "Are you joining us for tea?" Otto asked, aiming the question at Everett and George. He knew he would be waiting all day for Arnold to ask as he just didn't have the same confidence as Otto.

"Erm, if that's ok?" Everett replied, despite George looking less than impressed at her for accepting the invitation.

"That would be great," Arnold said, feeling pleased that Otto had asked but even happier that Everett had accepted. They walked back down the road, still talking about the film and Otto protesting the reasons why it made such a good cinematic experience. Before long they had reached the train station.

The weather suddenly turned; it began to rain so heavily, they had to run the last hundred yards to get to the shelter on the train platform. Everett shuddered from the cold and huddled into George to keep herself warm. Otto shook his head like you would see a dog shake themselves when ridding themselves of any excess water that they had in their fur.

"Where did that come from?" Otto asked as he finished shaking his head. The rain was bouncing off the floor and the noise from the rain hitting the shelter was incredibly loud. It sounded as if stones were being thrown at it rather than rain. Arnold felt it was quite therapeutic and he found himself looking out across the field opposite them on the other side of the train station in an almost hypnotic state.

As he stared, something caught his eye at the far corner of the field. Arnold focused his eyes and could see an old man carrying his shopping bag and another man in a long overcoat stood opposite him. They seemed to be staring at each other.

"That's odd," Arnold spoke out loudly to the others. The others were confused by what he had just said.

"What's odd, Arnold?" Everett asked, walking over to Arnold, trying to follow his eyes. Arnold pointed out to the field in front of them.

"Over there. Two men are staring at each other". Arnold directed his friends' attention to the far corner of the field, next to a footpath. Everyone looked across but could only just make out two shapes, but they could not tell if they were people or that they were staring at each other.

"You ok Arnold? Can't really see much." Otto was squinting his eyes, attempting to improve what he could see but the combination of the distance and the torrential rain made this impossible. Everett and George also confirmed that they could not make out what Arnold was pointing too, either.

Arnold looked over again, confused as to why it was so clear to him and not to the others; he could see clear as day an elderly man with a flat cap on stood opposite a man with a long black coat. As Arnold focused more on the man with the overcoat on, he saw him pull something from his jacket. Arnold recoiled, and a feeling of horror came over him as he realised that the man had pulled a blade from underneath his jacket and was running towards the elderly man. Without thinking, Arnold stepped forward jumping down onto the track before climbing up the other side, scaling the fence and dropping down into the field at speed. Arnold had not thought about this; he was acting purely on instinct and because of this had absolutely no idea what he was going to do when he reached the man with the blade. Arnold just knew he needed to get to the far corner of the field to help the man that was clearly in danger. He found it difficult to cover ground as the rain had made it a combination of slippy and muddy. His legs soon became heavy as his trainers and jeans became filthy with the tar-like mud that clung to his legs. He felt as though his chest was going to explode his heart was pounding that much and the rain was lashing against his face, the stinging sensation like needles, stabbing into his skin. A bright flash lit up the darkened sky in front of him, followed by an almighty roar like he had never heard before. His ears began to echo from the noise and somehow, he instantly knew that a powerful spirit beast had been summoned.

Over his shoulder, Arnold could hear the muffled sound of the others calling. They had followed him across the track and into the field without a moment's hesitation. In no time, Otto had caught up with Arnold as he was much faster. They had made good ground, and by this point, the others could also see what was unfolding in the corner of the field. An elderly man was slumped on the floor whilst the man in the overcoat engaged in combat with a spirit beast, a large battle-worn hippo. The spirit beast stood its ground with its mouth open baring its large, razor-sharp teeth. This did not appear to phase the man, who simply ran at the beast and jumped into the air over the top of it, plunging his blade into its back. The hippo let out an almighty roar and slumped to the floor; the man walked over and retrieved his blade from the spirit beast's back.

'How is that?' Arnold thought, knowing that no ordinary weapon should be able to interact with a spirit beast. The elderly man let out a groan, clearly feeling the pain of his spirit beast he was linked to. The hippo let out a low moan and began to absorb back into the body of the elderly man. The man in the overcoat walked towards the elderly man with a crooked smile on his face, holding the blade in front of him.

"Give me your power!" The man was angry, his outstretched arm holding the blade tightly. Arnold could see a glow of light emitting from the elderly man and watched as it moved towards the man in the overcoat. Arnold realised he was absorbing the old man's spirit beast, but how? He was suddenly distracted by the soft glow of the fox and boar spirit beasts that were running past him; they were making easy ground on the difficult terrain. The boar and the fox ran straight at the man in the overcoat, the fox leaping through the air and into the back of the man. The boar then followed this up by charging into the back of his legs, causing their target to lose his balance. He lost his footing and fell onto the muddy ground. Otto and Arnold began shouting to get the man's attention, which worked. He quickly got to his feet; a look of utter hatred drawn into his features.

"Fools," he growled. "You have no idea what you are doing." He began to walk towards them at a pace.

"Now what?" Arnold whispered to Otto under his breath, still trying to regulate his breathing after the sprint across the field. Otto glanced back at Arnold.

"Run."

The pair set off running again, knowing that they had the full attention of the attacker. The next thing Arnold knew, the darkness behind them was illuminated. The light flooded the immediate area around them as though it was daylight, a supernatural glow pulsating from within the area. There was a sudden density to the air, an unnatural feel around them. Arnold heard a deafening roar that shook him to the core, and he felt something strike the back of him, knocking him to floor with considerable force. Winded, Arnold began to pick himself up from the floor. He looked over to his side and noticed Otto had also been knocked to the ground, except Otto looked unconscious. Arnold looked around for what must have been the man's spirit beast, but he could not see it. All he could see was the scarred face of the man stood in front of him, his blade firmly in his grasp. The scars that engulfed his face left large, cracked indentations within his skin, showing his horrific disfiguration. Arnold had never known fear like it; he knew the man was going to kill him. His heart raced even faster than before and he felt lightheaded from the adrenaline that was coursing through his body.

"You sucker-punched me. How dare you!" he growled, his aggression every bit as intimidating as he intended it to be. "You interrupted me and now you will face the consequences of your petulance". The scarred man looked furious; he did not appreciate this unexpected delay. He lashed out and struck Arnold across the face, before grabbing the back of his collar and directing another heavy blow against his head. Arnold had never been struck before; he never wanted to again as his head began instantly throbbing and his vision blurring. He felt as though his brain had been rattled from the blow and as he gathered himself, he could feel his cheek burning from the first blow and the warm sensation of blood flowing down his face.

"You think that your pathetic, tiny insignificant spirit beasts will be able to stop me and save him?" the scarred man said through gritted teeth, leaning forward and grabbing Arnold by the scruff of his neck. He picked him up from the floor with ease, almost like he didn't weigh a thing. "You think you are saving a poor defenceless man? You know NOTHING. This does not concern you". He cocked his head to one side and sneered. "Well, it didn't." Arnold stared the scarred man in the face as he was hoisted in the air. He began to flail as he tried to escape his grasp, but it was to no avail; he was at the mercy of the scarred man. Pulling back his blade, he readied himself to finish Arnold off but then he caught him glancing over his shoulder. "Something distracting you?" he sneered, clearly incensed by Arnold's persistent petulance.

"Those spirit beasts weren't ours," Arnold said, nodding towards the elderly man. The scarred man looked back over his shoulder to see Everett and George tending to him. Arnold swung his leg back and aimed a kick at the scarred man, making contact with his stomach. The scarred man let out a scream of rage and threw Arnold through the air, making him ricochet off the ground for several yards. He came to an abrupt stop as he rolled into a tree, his arms were trembling as he attempted to pick himself up from the ground. Arnold looked across the field and could see the flashing lights of the Doyens arriving. Arnold struggled to his feet, waiting for the next blow but it didn't happen. Instead, Otto had thrown himself onto the back of the attacker and was frantically holding on as if trying to choke him. He was easily thrown off him, however, and was sent Arnold's way, with the two of them crashing together. Arnold gathered himself and anticipated another blow, but it didn't happen. The scarred man had simply vanished. Arnold hobbled over to Otto to check he was ok and as he reached him, Otto was coming to.

"What happened?" Otto sat himself up, holding the back of his head. He had a nasty looking claw mark on his shoulder. He grimaced as he put his hand over his shoulder and then looked to see his hand covered in blood. Arnold knelt to support him.

"I think we just saved that old man's life." Arnold pointed to Everett and George who were sat on the floor with the old man. Arnold could see George pointing and shouting towards them, directing Arnold's dad to where they were. He and another Doyen set off running towards them, and Otto looked up at Arnold.

"Your dad is going to kill us," he groaned, as he slouched back into Arnold's arms.

"He won't. I think we did well."

Chapter Six

"And you are sure that's everything that you can remember, Arnold?" Arthur was stood next to him in the hospital bay, waiting for the doctor to come and give Arnold the once over.

"I've told you everything, Dad." He had lost count of how many times he had gone over what had happened. He knew he had to, but with his head feeling like it had been split in two, he was becoming a little frustrated at having to repeat himself. "Is the old man ok? Do you know who he is?"

Arthur shuffled around nervously; he seemed to have more than one thing on his mind. Arthur was the highest-ranking Doyen in the area, meaning that everyone would be looking at him for answers.

"The old man is called Charles and he is not in a good way. As it stands, he is in a coma and he is not responding." Arthur sat in the chair that was next to Arnold's bed. "Are you absolutely certain that you saw Charles' spirit beast beaten by a man who had not summoned their spirit beast? Are you certain that it looked like the attacker was absorbing Charles' spirit beast?" His dad looked deep in thought, clearly disturbed by the night's events.

"I know what I saw, Dad. The scarred man was fighting with the spirit beast and when he beat it, he began to draw it from the old man as he lay on the floor. He was using his blade." Arnold sighed. He just wanted to rest; he felt so tired and he was having to fight to keep his eyes open.

"So he had an artefact? A vessel to transfer the old man's spirit beast to use as his own? If this is true, then we must inform the council immediately. The Chichen have most artefacts and they have them for reasons like this. Menials cannot be trusted with the power that these artefacts can bestow." Arthur spoke quickly, his thoughts spilling out of his mouth as fast as they were entering his head.

"You have no idea how lucky you are, Arnold. How you managed to not get yourself killed is beyond me, especially if the man was able to fight a spirit beast on his own. That itself shows how powerful he must be."

"I just wanted to help, Dad. I couldn't leave an old man there being attacked."

"I'm proud of you son, honestly I am. You have shown incredible bravery when others would have run. It could have gone so wrong, though" His dad appeared to shudder at the thought of losing his son. "I don't know what, you know if you-"

"I understand, Dad," Arnold said while smiling.

At this point, the blue curtains that surrounded Arnold's bay were drawn back, the metal hoops scraping against the rail that kept the curtains fixed to the ceiling.

"Master Ethon, my name is Doctor Sanj. I am here to give you a once over. Is it ok if I call you Arnold?" Her voice was soft and reassuring.

"Sure." Doctor Sanj pulled out a small torch from her dark blue scrub top and shone it in Arnold's eyes to check for signs of concussion. Arthur's phone began to ring, and he gestured to Arnold that he needed to take the call, leaving the bay to answer it.

Doctor Sanj raised a finger. "Ok, Arnold, can you follow my hand?" She began to slowly move her hand from one side to another. Arnold focused on her finger, following the instructions he had been given. "You have a mild concussion. Nothing a few days rest won't put right.

I will let your parents know that you will need a few days off school to recover."

"Sorry Doctor Sanj, did you say parents?" Arnold knew instantly what was coming.

"Where is he? Is he here?" The woman's panicked voice was instantly recognizable to Arnold.

It was his mum and he knew what was coming next. She burst into the bay hurriedly, her face pale and gaunt with worry.

"Goodness look at you!" she gasped, her eyes filling with tears. Her cheeks were blotchy from where she had been crying with worry. Grabbing hold of Arnold, she squeezed him so tightly, he thought that his head was about to pop. She pulled away from him and moved his head to one side to give him a quick once over herself, revealing the cut on his head that had been stitched. "What were you thinking?" Arthur walked back into the bay.

"Eve, give the boy some breathing space. You are going to suffocate him." She sat down in the chair next to Arnold and took hold of his hand, squeezing it tightly. Dr Sanj turned to face Arnold's parents.

"Mr. and Mrs. Ethon, Arnold will be fine to go home soon; we just want to finish these observations. He needs to rest, and I will prescribe him some pain killers. You should both be very proud of him; he has saved someone's life."

"We are, thank you, doctor," Eve said, smiling wearily.

"I will be back shortly with the pain killers and then Arnold is free to go."

"Thanks, Doctor," said Arthur. "I've just been to check on Otto. He is fine but he's had stitches for the slash he received on his shoulder. It must have been the scarred man's spirit beast that did this as it is a claw mark. He is luckier than you are if he was attacked by a spirit beast." Arthur placed his hand on Arnold's shoulder. "Mr. Whitaker is here, and he wants to speak to you."

Arnold knew Mr. Whitaker was his dad's boss but felt slightly confused as to why he would come and visit him at the hospital. At that moment, Arnold could hear a well-spoken male voice coming from behind the curtain. "I'm looking for Ethon".

Arthur left the cubicle and returned with Mr. Whitaker and a woman with whom he was unfamiliar. Mr. Whitaker was taller than his dad and dressed very smartly with his purple shirt standing out from his dark pin-striped suit. His slicked back, blonde hair making him look more like a banker than someone who worked for the Chichen. The woman had a somewhat nervous disposition and was dressed as though she had come straight from the office, her red and white floral blouse tucked neatly into her skirt and her blonde hair bobbed to her shoulders. She looked quite young to be working in the Chichen as Arnold presumed that the woman was in her twenties.

"Arnold, this is Mr. Whitaker and Miss Rushton. Mr. Whitaker is my senior at the Chichen, and Miss Rushton is the regional secretary."

"Please call me Sue," the woman said, her softly spoken voice reassuring Arnold whose nerves were beginning to set in now that his dad's boss was here to see him. "Mr. Whitaker has something he wishes to discuss with you," Sue continued. "How are you feeling?"

"I'm ok," Arnold replied. "Cracking headache, though." He raised his hand up to his head. Sue placed her hand reassuringly on Arnold's arm and cast him a warm smile. Arnold knew straight away that he liked her and took comfort from her smile. Mr. Whitaker let out a subtle cough to capture Sue's attention, who withdrew her hand straight away and stepped back from Arnold, allowing him to take a step forward to stand next to him.

"The old man that you saved is called Charles Grey and he used to be a Doyen, a very powerful one. Not only did you and your friends save his life, but you also stopped his spirit beast from being stolen. What's worrying is that this attacker, who is most likely a menial, has in his possession an artefact that we are unaware of. This is why the Chichen likes to keep hold of artefacts, to stop them from falling into the wrong hands. Rest assured our resources are now extended to finding this mad man and acquiring the blade he has," Mr. Whitaker said, his well-spoken voice matching the expensive-looking suit that he was wearing.

"But I think he had a spirit beast so how can he be a menial?" Arnold asked.

"Because of the artefact he had in his possession," Mr Whitaker responded. "Did you see what he summoned?" Arnold shook his head.

"No, sir. All I remember was the darkness lighting up behind me and the roar from whatever chased us."

"I see. Well if you do remember any more details, make sure you tell us. We might be able to figure out what the artefact he had, was." Mr. Whitaker continued "Now, enough of the small talk let's get to the real reason that I am here. We, and by that I mean the Chichen, would like to extend an invitation for you to join."

"I'm sorry, what?" Arnold frowned, thinking he must have misheard Mr. Whitaker. "You're asking me to join the Chichen?" His heart began to race. He must be dreaming, or his concussion was setting in. Joining the Chichen was what he had wanted for his entire life. "But I'm only fifteen?"

"Not just you. Your friends that all assisted have been invited, too," Mr. Whitaker said, "Although the two girls, was it Everett and Georgina? They declined."

"How are we allowed in the Chichen?" Arnold asked, unable to process what he was being told.

"A loop-hole" Sue responded, not entirely confident in her words. The look that Mr. Whitaker gave her reaffirmed this lack of confidence.

"I do not agree with this, however, the Chichen have instructed me to extend an invitation to you." Mr. Whitaker moved his hands behind his back before continuing. "In saving the life of a Doyen, you have earned the right to this invitation. It does not mean that you will be successful especially given that the expectations are extremely high and from what I understand you do not yet have a spirit beast. To be in the Chichen without a spirit beast is most irregular." Arnold could tell that Mr. Whitaker was not fully on board, but he did not care. He had just received an invitation to join the Chichen and despite his horrific headache, this was the best day of his life. "Should you accept, I expect you to arrive at the Chichen next Monday, following the end of your school day. That should give you sufficient time to recover". Mr. Whitaker turned to leave the cubicle where Arnold now sat in utter shock. "Arthur, I will see you in the morning for a debrief," he added as he left. Sue cast another warm smile at Arnold as she hurried to follow her boss and leave the hospital.

Arnold beamed at his dad, but Arthur did not appear to be as happy as his son was at the news he had just received.

"I'm happy for you because I know what this means to you. However, I know what you will have to go through to join and I do feel you are too young for this. It is your decision, Arnold. If you join, we can train you on how to defend yourself. In case he comes back."

A sudden wave of panic came over Arnold and his heart felt heavy. "Do you think he will come after us?"

"It's the main reason I would want you to join," Arthur responded. "At least if you start to receive some training, you may be able to harness your spirit beast and defend yourself if he was to show up again."

"I don't have a spirit beast though so how can I join the Chichen if I could still be a menial?" Arnold's mind began to race with reasons why joining the Chichen might fail.

"You are forgetting one important thing Arnold; your spirit beast has started to manifest." Arnold stared blankly; he had no idea what his dad was talking about. "You said you could see right across the field as clear as anything when nobody else could. You could see everything that was happening from a lot further than you should have been able to." The blank expression on Arnold's face began to melt away as he slowly began to understand where his dad was going with this. "You have enhanced vision, Arnold, and that's quite a rare attribute to develop." Arnold felt as though a huge weight had been lifted off him. Finally, his spirit beast was starting to manifest! All he needed to do now was research what spirit beasts could be linked to him having enhanced vision. "You need to rest now, son. You've had quite an eventful birthday." Arthur patted his son's arm. "The doctors are happy for you to come home with me. Just have a think over the next couple of days about Mr. Whitakers offer."

Arnold spent the next 24 hours in his own bed, sleeping. He had the worst headache he had ever experienced, a symptom of the concussion from his encounter with the scarred man. His mum crept into his room to check on him from time to time and to ensure he was drinking enough water. She was also trying her hardest to get him to eat some food, but he did not have the appetite for anything.

It was well into the night when Arnold was awoken by muffled voices coming from downstairs. He checked his alarm clock by the side of his bed to see that it was just after midnight. Arnold was instantly confused, wondering who would be calling at his house at this time. In a daze, Arnold got out of his bed and walked across his bedroom, stopping momentarily when a head rush kicked in after his sudden movement. Once he had gathered himself, he crept across the landing to the top of the stairs to try and see who was in the house. As Arnold came around from his concussed sleep the two voices became clearer; one was his dad and the other was his grandad. He began to listen to their conversation.

"Arthur, I am telling you that the boy is too young to go. He may have shown he has enhanced vision but that is not enough, not for the level of training that he will be exposed to. It's too soon." His grandad's tone was assertive, almost slightly hostile towards his dad. "What if his spirit beast is a-" The floor creaked where Arnold stood so he didn't hear what his grandad said. "You know what I mean Arthur. The Chichen will take him away if they were to find out."

"Dad it's not entirely my decision," Arthur answered. "He needs to learn to defend himself and to harness his spirit beast. We can't be fully sure what it is yet; we are just guessing." His grandad shook his head in disagreement.

"But it could be. He has been having dreams of flying. Just like your Mum used to."

"I know Dad, but it's too risky even to discuss, especially if anyone realised what his abilities could be." There was a nervousness in his dad's voice that brought a fresh worry to Arnold. What had he not told him when he was in the hospital?

"Have you gone into detail with him yet? About his dreams and what they could mean?" his grandad quizzed.

"Not yet. The timing isn't right. He has been asking questions, but I need to know for sure that his dreams and ability are linked."

"He needs to know Arthur. Not only would it be hard to master but there is a large chance that he could be corrupted. You don't need me to go into detail about that again. Need I remind you of your mum and what it did to her?" There was a pain in his Grandad's voice that Arnold did not like; it croaked and wavered as he spoke about his grandma. Arnold didn't know anything about her, so his curiosity was instantly heightened. He leaned in closer to the stairs, not wanting to miss anything that was said.

"You don't need to remind me, Dad. I lived through it with you." His dad's voice began to raise, an air of frustration in his response. "I grew up without her, because of it. Arnold is a good boy; whatever his spirit beast is he will still be a good boy and for that reason alone he shouldn't be told yet. Not until he is ready. I don't want it to influence him." Arnold felt intrigued by his dad's comments; what was so bad that they couldn't just tell him? What did they think his spirit beast was and what on earth had happened to his grandma? "I don't want people to judge him for his spirit beast, not because of history." His dad was taking an assertive stance with his grandad. "We will have to see how he develops, if there are any signs, I will get him out of the Chichen before anyone even realises."

"He needs to know, Arthur. You say you want to prepare him but how can he be prepared if he doesn't even know about what happened all those years ago? It's part of our family's history and if you won't tell him then I will. I can't just stand here and do nothing. Not after your mum. The boy needs to be ready."

"Then you need to give him some space while I try and figure this out. He is my son and I will protect him how I see fit!" Arnold's dad slammed his hand down on the coffee table that was next to him.

His grandad looked saddened at his dad's comments, clearly hurt by the command that he had just issued with.

"He's too young for the training, Arthur. Please think about this - he is just a boy." Fighting back tears, his grandad continued "He is my grandson, my only grandchild, and I believe he needs to know, and I feel it is too soon to train him. The Ch'ahb', it's traumatic. It might change him."

"I can't go against the will of the Chichen. He has been invited and if he doesn't go now then I don't think they will offer it again when he is older. The council does not take too kindly to being rejected."

Arthur looked pleadingly at his dad, hoping he would see sense. He didn't.

"That isn't a bad thing, Arthur." He looked astonished.

"How can you say that!? You were an Elder before you retired." Arnold's Grandad sighed.

"I have my reasons. I have respected your decision to join the Chichen but that doesn't mean I agree with Arnold joining."

"He isn't being told about Mum and he certainly isn't being told about his spirit beast. We will deal with that when he finds out what it is. All we will do is worry him if we tell him now. I'm not going to change my mind so I think you should leave." There was a shortness to his dad's words, a coldness in his voice that strongly suggested he was serious about what he was saying. Arnold's grandad turned and shuffled to the front door and left without another word being spoken. Arnold felt a surge of anger inside him that was overpowering; he had never felt anything like it before. He contemplated challenging his dad but decided against this, seeing that he was already keeping secrets from him.

Arnold crept back to his bedroom, trying as hard as he could to not make any noise and draw attention to himself. "How dare he," Arnold muttered to himself while pacing in his bedroom, still unsure what to make of everything he had heard., After ranting to himself for the best part of an hour, Arnold got back in bed, his mind still whirling with questions and his head spinning with his concussion. What spirit beast were they referring to? What had happened to his grandma? Why was his grandad worried about the Chichen when he had been an Elder there? These were the questions that Arnold was asking himself; questions he desperately wanted answers to.

Chapter Seven

Arnold remained in his bed for the next two days as he continued his recovery from the concussion, though in part he did not leave his room as he didn't want to see his dad. Arthur had thrown himself into work and Arnold knew it was because of his disagreement with his grandad. As it stood, he hadn't told his dad about anything he had overheard. Arthur had come home from work late the last two nights after leaving unusually early. Arnold did not feel bad about this; he was frustrated by the secrets being kept from him and didn't feel he was ready to talk to him yet anyway. Sadly, this didn't lessen his need to know the answers to his many questions.

He planned to see his grandad, but since the attack his mum had kept him under strict observation, meaning he wasn't able to sneak out of the house. Arnold was sat on his bed reading, finally able to undertake the arduous task now that his concussion was pretty much gone. The book in question was 'Spirit Beasts; Unlocking Your Potential'. It was a self-help guide from his favourite spirit beast expert, Davies Gregor. Arnold had most of his books and envied that he got to travel the world, exploring the histories behind different cultures and their ancient links to spirit beasts. Arnold was busy scribbling notes in his pad trying to link realistic ways that he could trigger his spirit beast manifestation. Whilst scribbling down key words, his bedroom door creaked open and his mum poked her head into the room.

"Otto is here to see you," she said, stepping back to let him into the room. "I thought a visit might cheer you up." Otto entered the room and smiled.

"How's the head?"

"Sore. How's the shoulder?" Arnold replied, putting his pad back on the bedside table.

"Not as painful now. As soon as I was back from the hospital, my Mum and Dad put one of the traditional family remedies on the wound and the pain hasn't been that bad since. My dad reckons it's a claw mark from a spirit beast in the cat category." Turning around, Otto lifted his t-shirt to reveal the 4 gashes on his shoulder that covered a good portion of his back. The thick stitches that had been inserted to pull the skin together and reduce scarring were visible through the dark green, thick mixture of herbs that his parents had rubbed into the wound. He lowered his t-shirt with a goofy look on his face "Pretty cool, eh?"

"Looks pretty sore. Did your dad say what type of big cat?"

"No, only a specialist would know and there were none available at the hospital because, let's face it, this kind of spirit beast attack never happens."

"I wonder if my dad or someone at the Chichen could help? Did my dad speak to you and your parents about the offer from Mr. Whitaker?" Arnold scanned Otto's face to see if he could see what decision he had made.

"Yeah."

"Everett and George have said they don't want to accept the invite. I can't believe they wouldn't take up the offer. This is such a great opportunity."

"Not everyone is as keen on the Chichen as you, Arnold," Otto smirked. "I said yes though. Think about it - they both have their spirit beasts whereas we don't. They are both more advanced than both of us put together." Otto continued to go into detail. "It's only because of the tradition that we are allowed in as we challenged the scarred man and came out alive. We challenged someone who was considerably stronger than us to save the old man despite the danger to us. Speaking of which – how is the old guy?" Arnold shrugged.

"Not sure. My mum said he is still in a coma and he is not showing any signs of waking up. His spirit beast was stabbed so that must have really hurt."

Otto threw himself into the bean bag in the centre of Arnold's bedroom then grimaced at the pain that he had felt in his shoulder. "My dad reckons that there is something we are not being told by the Doyens. Keeps asking me about what we saw because normal weapons cannot interact with Spirit beasts, only certain artefacts can."

"That's another question that my dad needs to answer, then." Arnold suddenly felt that it was time to start asking the questions he had, as they were mounting up. Arnold swung his legs out of his bed and placed his feet on the floor.

"Do you know what else is interesting? There hasn't been a single story on the news or in the local paper about what happened," Otto said, pulling a copy of the Oswald Advertiser from his rucksack.

"Doesn't surprise me, my dad is good at keeping secrets at the minute." There was a bitterness to Arnold's voice caused by the resentment he was currently experiencing towards his dad. Of course, this went straight over Otto's head and he had no idea what Arnold was on about, so Arnold spent the next 20 minutes filling Otto in on the conversation he had overheard between his dad and grandad.

"The plot thickens...do you actually think that your dad will stop you from seeing your grandad?" Otto asked, slouching into the bean bag whilst taking in everything that Arnold was telling him.

"He can try. I would just go around anyway. I have too many questions that need answering and I think I'm more likely to get them from my grandad than my dad." Arnold was already planning in his head that he would go and visit his grandad one day after school this week. He'd had to take a few days off following the events from his birthday. Arnold felt glad that he had not had to go into school for the last few days as he would have struggled to concentrate with his mild concussion but also, he could not stop thinking about what he had heard his grandad say. He felt that both his grandad and dad knew what his spirit beast was and that it could be linked to a spirit beast that hasn't been around for a long time. Arnold was also wondering about his grandma and how she was involved.

There was another knock at the front door, followed by the sound of footsteps rushing up the stairs. Everett and George came bundling into the room and rushed towards Arnold and Otto, wrapping their arms around them and giving them hugs.

"Ow careful!" Otto scolded Everett who had inadvertently caught his shoulder, causing a nauseating pain to engulf him.

"Sorry, we just wanted to see you guys! We were told to leave you for a few days and we just wanted to make sure you were both ok." Everett then switched over to Arnold and gave him an equally restrictive hug. Otto proceeded to fill Everett and George in on everything that they had just been discussing and answered the same questions that he had asked a short time ago.

"This is so messed up; I mean, who does that to an old man? To see his poor spirit beast stabbed like that was awful. I had no idea that you can be so in tune with your spirit beast that you feel the pain that it feels," George said. She felt even more strongly about spirit beast rights now. "Do you think it might work the other way around? Where the spirit beast feels the pain of their anchor?" George asked with a determined look on her face which implied she now had a new theory to research.

"What about the scarred man?" Everett asked. Arnold shrugged, unable to give any further information on him.

"Apparently the Doyens are searching for him, but they have no idea who he is or what his motive is. He's just vanished into thin air. I guess no one will know until the old man wakes up." He had a horrible feeling deep down about the scarred man; what if his dad was right and there was a chance that he would come after them for interfering? After all, they had stopped him from killing the old man. "We need to be prepared if he comes back for us."

"That's why we need to go to the Chichen," Otto added.

"I take it you guys have accepted the invitation then?" Everett asked.

"They asked us, too, but it's just not for us. Besides, I'm too busy helping out at my Granny's shop," said George, referring to the home remedies store that her Granny ran in town where she also practiced as a traditional healer. This was something that George intended to pursue so the Chichen held little interest for her. Otto continued.

"I was just telling Arnold that they have really strict values and traditions which we have met on a technicality. Arnold told them he wouldn't join because he didn't think you guys had been invited."

"Did you really say that, Arnold? That's so sweet," Everett beamed. Arnold looked around the room sheepishly, his cheeks becoming a rose colour that he was becoming too accustomed to whenever he was around Everett.

"Well, we were all there. We all helped."

"That's cute, Arnold, but this is far too big of an opportunity for you. Me and George have other plans. I want to go to university for starters."

"It is a great opportunity for you two though. You should totally go for it," George added.

"Erm ok then, I will speak to my dad when he gets home later." Arnold felt grateful to Everett for giving her blessing as it had helped with the internal conflict he had been feeling. "We need to be prepared for if the scarred man comes back." It was the one thing that Arnold did agree with his dad on. "We need to go to the Chichen to keep ourselves safe."

"My parents have said I can go. My dad wasn't so keen though - keeps harping on about family tradition," Otto said, rolling his eyes. He had never really taken his dad's ramblings about family tradition too seriously. George looked down at her watch. "I don't know about you guys, but I need to head home for tea." Otto and Everett agreed and the three of them left Arnold's bedroom together. Arnold sat on his bean bag waiting for tea and for his dad to get home.

About one hour later, Arnold was sat with his mum at the dinner table making his way through the lasagna that she had made them all for their tea. Arnold leaned forward to pick up a piece of garlic bread from the centre of the table.

"Dad's home late again." He knew he needed to speak with his dad but couldn't help putting a dig in against him. Arnold's mum let out a sigh, disheartened at the way that Arnold was being with his dad.

"You two need to sort this out. You're both just as stubborn as each other." She continued, "He should not have spoken to your grandad as he did, but he just wants to protect you. He really thinks you should go to the Chichen with him." Arnold hadn't said a word to his mum but still she had put two and two together as to why Arnold had been so awkward around his dad recently. Arnold took a bite out of the garlic bread that he had just picked up.

"I have decided I will go, but I have questions that need answering".

"Make sure you talk to your dad when he gets home." At that moment, the front door opened, and Arnold's dad entered the house.

"Nice of you to join us," Arnold sniped. He may need to speak with his dad, but he was still mad at him.

"Arnold!" His mum scolded him. "Don't speak to your dad like that". Arnold didn't get told off often, but he knew he just overstepped the mark.

The next fifteen minutes felt incredibly uncomfortable, as the family finished the lasagna and garlic bread without speaking a word. After they finished, Arnold cleared the table and went through to the kitchen to clean the dishes.

"Need a hand, son?" His dad's voice came from behind him as he stood with his hands in the washing up bowl. His dad walked over and picked up the folded tea towel that was neatly placed over the handle of the oven and began drying the dishes that Arnold had washed. Arnold fixed his gaze on the bowl, choosing not to engage in conversation. He knew he had questions and that he needed to speak with his dad to get answers, but he did not know how to respond to him because of the frustration he was feeling. His dad continued, despite Arnold's reluctance to talk to him. "I am just trying to protect you, Arnold. You are not ready to know everything yet. You are too young; I was eighteen before your grandad told me everything." His face looked pained and Arnold did not know how to respond. "Your dreams are suggesting you may be manifesting a certain type of spirit beast and I've not wanted to tell you this as I don't want it to influence you. I want you to be able to connect to your spirit beast naturally." Arthur sighed. "Well, to a certain extent, if you accept the offer, your training will boost your connection as nothing else can. If I told you what I thought your spirit beast was it could delay or change how it manifests, by changing the way you respond to things." His dad put the tea towel down and walked over to a barstool and put his head in his hands. "I didn't mean to speak to your grandad like I did and I feel terrible for it. We both want what is best for you, but we just have different ways that we feel is the best way to help and support you." Arnold turned around to face his dad.

"What happened to grandma? And is it linked to whatever spirit beast you think I might have?" Arnold had asked the questions before he had time to think.

"It's not my place to tell you what happened to your grandma, but yes - I do think your spirit beast might be linked; it is too much of a coincidence for my liking. If you want to know what happened to your grandma, you need to speak with grandad. I don't think you are ready, but I will respect your right to ask." Arthur stood up again, walked back to the sink and picked up his tea towel. "Your grandad has gone away for a week or so to clear his head. After everything that has happened, he said he needs to be somewhere that is not here to think." Arthur put his hand on his son's shoulder. "When he gets back Arnold, I promise you – you can speak to him and ask all the questions you want." Arnold believed his dad but was now intrigued as to where his grandad had gone. Arthur patted his son's shoulder. "You and Otto need to come to the Chichen with me. Only there can you be taught how to truly master your spirit beast, whatever it may be. Starting tomorrow, you need to come every day after school. It will not be easy for either of you; the training is gruelling and you two are very young to begin it. It is unheard of for children your age to be invited but we have to honour tradition." Arnold's dad sounded apprehensive with his words as if he wasn't fully sure that they should be joining him at the Chichen. "Then there is the Ch'ahb.'"

"You mentioned that. What is it?" Arnold asked.

"It will be your initiation, a ceremony that all invited to train in the Chichen have to go through. That is all I can tell you."

"What will happen?" Arnold's previous anger towards his dad was melting away as his fascination with the Chichen overrode it.

"Arnold, I can't tell you. It could alter the ritual."

Disappointed but totally understanding his dad's position, Arnold left it there and took himself off to his bedroom. Speaking with his dad had brought on feelings of excitement and nervousness about what he was going to experience at the Chichen. He was going to go inside the building he had always dreamed of entering and not only that, he was going to begin his training so much earlier than he ever imagined. Arnold lay on his bed, his thoughts jumping from the scarred man, the old man, his grandad, grandma and joining the Chichen. He still had so many questions and a part of him felt that he may not get all the answers he wanted, but at least for now he was getting somewhere. Arnold kept thinking about his spirit beast and how it somehow linked him to his grandma until eventually, he drifted off to sleep.

He was flying again but this time something felt different, he felt different. He felt bigger, more powerful and his wings felt larger than usual. He seemed to be covering ground a lot faster as his large, black wings propelled him through the air with ease. It felt sensational! Looking below at the fast-moving ground beneath him he could see his large shadow, but he was unable to make out his shape. This was not the same animal that he normally dreamt about, but he could feel the power he had was much more than what he usually experienced. Looking out across the vast fields in front of him he could see a large hill and sat at the top was a building that felt familiar to him. Focusing on the building, he continued to head in the direction of the building, covering ground at an incredible pace and much faster than what he was used to. The feeling was exhilarating and the adrenaline that was pumping through his body made him feel as though nothing could stop him.

As he reached the building, he adapted the position of his wings to start bringing himself to a halt, before gliding down to bring himself closer. Now at a slow glide, he could see the stone tower clearly in front of him surrounded by broken, rickety fences that looked as though a strong gust of wind would blow them over. The tower looked old and untidy, the dark grey stones had green moss creeping up to them from the ground, covering three-quarters of the building. Its windows were sealed from the inside with big, rusted metal panels that prevented anyone from looking inside. A large chimney protruded from the triangular roof that looked as though it was ready to collapse in on itself and there was another copper coloured sheet covering a small window, just below the chimney. Feeling drawn to the small window, he began to glide towards it but suddenly felt overcome with the sensation of falling as out of nowhere, he felt completely unable to fly. He began to hurtle towards the ground at speed, the rocks below fast approaching. He tucked his head low into his chest and wrapped his wings around himself, bracing himself for the impact.

Arnold woke up startled as he fell from his bed, his sheets were ruffled as though he had been flailing around like a koi carp that had jumped out of a pond. Arnold and his sheets were drenched with sweat and he sat bolt upright, quickly rising to instinctively grab his pad from his bedside drawers. He grabbed the pen he had clipped onto the pad and began to sketch the tower that he had just seen in his dream in as much detail as he could muster. Arnold was not the most talented artist, but he did the best he could and when he had finished, he sat staring at the tower that he had drawn. Arnold could not help but feel that this tower had something to do with his spirit beast and furthermore, he was certain that if he could find this tower it would help him manifest his spirit beast. He felt drawn to it, like a magnet. That tower had the answers he was looking for, he just knew it.

Chapter Eight

As soon as it was the morning, Arnold headed straight downstairs with his pad to show his dad his dream drawing. Arthur was already sat at the table making his way through his jam on toast.

"I had another dream last night," Arnold said, rushing across the room with his pad in his hand. "I saw something this time though. I've tried to sketch it in my pad - can you have a look at it?"

His dad put his toast to one side, reached out for the pad and took it from Arnold. Placing the pad down on the table he then opened it up to look at his drawing. He looked at the picture for a short while before closing the pad and sliding it back towards Arnold.

"Sorry son, I don't recognise it." Dejected, Arnold left his pad on the table and went back upstairs to get showered and ready for school. His mood lifted, however, as he prepared his school bag for the day's lessons. Today was the most special of days. Today was the day he was going to join the Chichen.

"Make sure you pack your gym clothes for after school," his mum called up the stairs. Arnold was so excited and could not wait to learn more about spirit beasts; all he had to do was make it through another day at school.

With his bag packed, Arnold came back downstairs and had some breakfast. As he finished off his cornflakes, his dad walked back into the room. "I'm heading off to the Chichen now," Arthur said, giving Arnold's mum a kiss as he made his way to the front door. His mum picked up his abandoned pad and placed it on some drawers in the hallway. Arthur left the room and Arnold could hear the front door close behind him as he set off for work. He finished off his cereal before he picked up his bowl and took it through to the kitchen.

"I'm leaving now." He placed his cereal bowl in the sink next to where his mum was.

"See you tonight, I hope everything goes well for you at the Chichen later." His mum spun around and gave Arnold a kiss on the head. "Trust your Dad."

Arnold quickly ran upstairs to grab his backpack and gym clothes before running down the stairs and straight out of the front door. Otto stood waiting for Arnold at the bottom of the path for their normal walk to school. "Today's the day! I can't wait for school to finish. Is it half three yet?" Otto joked as he put his hands in his pockets and set off walking next to Arnold. The two of them headed towards school to get the most boring part of the day done. The weather was matching Arnold's mood, bright and sunny. Today was going to be a good day.

"I had another dream last night. This was different though like I was something else. I felt more powerful than before...I felt like I was bigger? It was so strange. I saw this weird derelict tower with large stone walls which sat the top of a hillside," Arnold told Otto.

"You think it's a real building? Did you manage to draw it?" Arnold nodded answering both of Otto's questions in one head movement.

"I'm hoping it is real. Maybe it links to my spirit beast?" There was a hopefulness in Arnold's tone, he wanted it to be real so badly. The two continued on their journey to school.

They made it to school with Arnold filling in Otto with the rest of the details of his dream he could remember.

"So, it definitely felt different?" Otto asked.

"Yeah, this was not the same animal I normally dream of. It felt incredibly powerful, like nothing I have ever felt before. I felt angry, a real rage inside me that I could not get out of my system."

"Wait up!" The voice called out from behind them and Arnold instantly recognised it as being George; her distinctly broad northern accent making her stand out from everyone else. She had her beany firmly planted on her head with the usual lock of red hair poking down at the front of her forehead.

"Ask her what she thinks?" Otto suggested.

"About what?" George asked.

"Arnold's latest dream - says he was flying again. Did we tell you?" Otto asked.

"Tell me what?" she said, frowning. Otto laughed to himself

"Clearly not. Arnold has super sight." Not appreciating the title that Otto had taken it upon himself to give to his new-found ability he corrected him.

"It's more like enhanced vision."

"That's different. Wonder what that could mean. What about an owl?" George suggested. Otto burst into laughter.

"Maybe you're a bat!"

"Bats use sonar, you moron," George corrected. "Ignore him, Arnold. There are lots of other spirit beasts this could be linked to."

"Like what?"

"Er, well maybe this is what we need to look into for you," George suggested. "Your auro is developing and you are showing signs. You know what comes next." Arnold was holding little hope in this but was just glad that he had shown some form of a sign. All he had to do now was figure out what his spirit beast was going to be. Arnold couldn't help but feel that this enhanced vision he had developed was a bit of a useless attribute and felt jealous that Otto had become more athletic.

"When did you get yours?" Arnold asked.

"My fox?"

"No, your squirrel," Otto teased. George rolled her eyes before answering Arnold's question.

"About six months ago, I guess. I noticed I had become better at gymnastics and about a month after that, she appeared to me when I was in the garden at home practicing. It was amazing." Arnold considered her answer.

"How long after you turned fifteen did it appear?"

"Er, about two months after my birthday," George answered, thinking back.

"Sweet! Mine must be due at any time then," Otto exclaimed.

The bell rang indicating that all the students needed to be in their form rooms so the three of them said their goodbyes and split up to go into their separate classrooms before the next bell rang. Arnold sighed to himself as he sat down. At least he would be able to start looking into this more when he started training at the Chichen tonight. Now more than ever, he wanted to know what his spirit beast was going to be.

The rest of the school day seemed to drag, as all Arnold could think of was getting to the Chichen. He had just tried to get on with it; got his head down and completed the work he needed to in lessons. Eventually, he had made it to the end of the day and Arnold stood by the entrance to the school just past the main gates, where he and Otto had agreed to meet up. Arnold had begun pacing, his nerves beginning to kick in with the anticipation of going to the Chichen. He looked at his watch for the tenth time wondering where Otto was, not that it wasn't common for Otto to be late.

"You will be fine." Arnold could hear laughter and saw Everett walking towards him. "You're making me nervous with all that pacing. You need to try and calm yourself down." Everett scrunched her hair back into a ponytail and fastened it into place with the bobble she had wrapped around her wrist.

"Are you sure you don't want to join us at the Chichen?" Arnold asked. He wanted to make sure that the two of them were absolutely certain about their decision.

"Honestly, it's not for me and George is more interested in following in her Granny's footsteps." George caught up with Everett and the two said their goodbyes to Arnold and Otto before they set off down the street, walking arm in arm.

"Ready to go?" Otto called out as he exited the maths building and greeted Arnold at the gates.

"Seriously?! I have been here fifteen minutes and you're asking me if I am ready?" Arnold could be amazed at times about how stupid his friend could be.

"Needed the loo. Nerves and all that." Otto caught up with Arnold, and the two of them set off in the direction of the Chichen, neither knowing what to expect when they got there.

Before long the two of them were stood at the entrance to the Chichen, staring up at the building that Arnold had wanted to walk into since he was a small child. Now the opportunity presented itself to him, his legs felt like they were made of lead and he was unable to take the initial steps he needed to move forward.

The main part of the building sat atop of the four sides of stairs made of large blocks of limestone. Within the steps of the Chichen there were carved hieroglyphs denoting the spirit beasts of fallen Doyens or Elders. It is considered the highest honour for those serving the Chichen, but one that no man or woman ever lived to see happen for this was only awarded upon their death. The large, circular oak door was inscribed with words from a language that he did not understand; the wording covering the entire outside edge of the door. In the centre of the door was a large symbol. Upon closer inspection, the symbol carved out of the door was the large rose that represented Lancashire. Sitting just below, as if climbing over the petals themselves, was an intricate bee. The carvings on the door were like nothing Arnold had ever seen before and he stood for a while admiring the workmanship that had gone into it. Suddenly, the door opened from the inside, pulling back and then rolling to the side in such a smooth motion that it hardly made a sound. This was expert workmanship at its finest.

"Don't just stand there, come on in." Stood behind the door was Arnold's dad, a proud smile greeting them both. Otto stepped forward first, with Arnold following closely behind. His chest was pounding, and Arnold was feeling even more nervous. He walked into the building with no idea what to expect next.

Stepping inside, he was taken aback at what he saw. Behind the amazing door was a pretty normal looking lobby. Just beyond the door were a few seats and then opposite them, a reception area. The black and white marble floor which resembled a chessboard was freshly polished causing the light to reflect from the expensive-looking, intricate chandelier above.

"It's modern!" Arnold exclaimed, amazed at what he could see and completely surprised.

Arthur burst into laughter "What were you expecting? Chairs made of stone?" He continued to laugh. "We have to update the building to keep it fresh. Don't worry though, we have all the traditional chambers at various points around the Chichen. You will see soon enough." He guided Arnold and Otto past the reception area. "Sue, you met Arnold at the hospital. This is his best friend Otto." The receptionist stopped what she was doing and gave them both a warm smile.

"Welcome to the Chichen, boys."

"She's fit," whispered Otto. Arnold sniggered and nudged Otto as the two of them grinned at each other. She was sat behind the desk, her blonde shoulder-length hair absolutely poker straight. Her eyes were fixed on her computer screen as she typed away on the keyboard without even looking down at it. The two of them waved and Sue glanced up to offer a smile to the two of them before returning to her work. Arnold's dad led them past the reception area and down the hallway, before stopping to open a door.

"Come on in, this is my office". He gestured for them to enter and then followed them inside. "Please take a seat." Arnold couldn't help but feel that this was very business-like, and they sat down in the two chairs that were placed opposite his dad's desk. "Right. I just wanted to go through what will be happening this evening," he said. "The first thing I am going to need you to do is to get changed out of your uniforms; I will show you where the changing rooms are shortly. There will be two tunics in there for you. Put these on in preparation for your Ch'ahb'. Now normally this intensifies the connection between you and your spirit beast but as you two do not know their forms yet, this process will aid you in discovering what they are. I don't fully know what will happen, as normally you have your spirit beast when we carry this out. Should be interesting."

"Ch'ahb'? Already?" Arnold knew that there would be an initiation at some point, but he thought they would at least be shown around first. He had read that there were different initiation ceremonies specific to each Chichen, however, none of the books had any details about what the initiation would entail. It was a secret saved only for those that joined. His nerves intensified; suddenly everything seemed even more real. They left their backpacks in the office and were then led further down the corridor to the changing rooms and his dad guided them inside.

"Your tunics are hanging up over there. Put them on and I will be waiting outside to take you up to the chamber where your initiation will take place," he explained.

His dad left the room, leaving them to get ready. At the other end of the changing room, two dark green tunics were hanging up just like his dad had told them.

"This just got a bit weird," Otto said, concern heavy in his voice.

"Everyone that's accepted into the Chichen has to do this. Even though I have no idea what this is." Arnold also felt that this was weird but decided he was ok to go along with it. He began to get undressed before picking up the tunic to examine it in more detail. The dark green material was stitched together with fine, gold thread. He looked at the front of the tunic and saw the same symbol that was on the front door embroidered onto it. It was the same rose and bee that was so beautifully carved into the door at the entrance. The two of them placed their tunics on and headed back out to the corridor where his dad was waiting for them. To Arnold's surprise, his dad had changed into a dark blue tunic which had the same symbol as theirs on, but his dad's tunic had more intricate embroidery on his sleeves, including four stripes on his right sleeve.

"It's my rank," Arthur said, noticing Arnold staring at his sleeve. "This way."

Arnold and Otto followed his dad down the hall before stopping again; this time it was a lift door that was in front of them. Pressing the button to call the lift, his dad stood silently, his hands crossed in front of him. The lift doors opened and the three of them walked in.

Arnold stood next to his dad wondering what was about to happen to them. "Where are we going?" he asked, his voice wavering as his nerves began to show.

"We are going to the chamber at the bottom of the Chichen. That is where the Ch'ahb' will take place." Arthur inputted a code into a keypad on the wall of the lift and the doors shut. The lift shuddered and then began to move. "If at any time you don't want to continue, just let us know and we will stop. What you are about to experience will hurt but it is all part of the process and it will not put your life in danger. I need you to trust me on that."

"What does Ch'ahb' mean?" Otto quizzed, taking the advice they were just given in his stride.

"You will know soon enough," Arthur replied.

"That's all you're going to say? Come on," Otto said, hoping for more information. Letting out a sigh, Arthur looked forward at the doors of the elevator.

"It translates as 'blood-letting." Arnold and Otto looked at each other, both with a slightly panicked expression. Arnold could feel his blood draining from his face as he stood waiting for the lift doors to open. Within a few moments, they did.

Chapter Nine

"I'm sorry, what?" Otto asked.

"It translates as blood-letting. Now follow me." They followed Arthur into the chamber which was dimly lit by flames placed all around the room. His tunic draped along the floor, sliding across the floor in a smooth motion that made it appear as though he was gliding across the chamber.

Arnold couldn't make out much of the room. He could see stone pillars lining up on either side of the chamber, each with what looked like their own intricate patterns inscribed. He stared intently to bring them into focus, to see what looked like faces cast into the stone; the lighting in the room was too poor to make out any specific details. Beyond the pillars all Arnold could see was darkness. Not knowing what was beyond the darkness, his attention was drawn to the centre of the chamber instead, where a man stood with a stone casket in front of him. The shadows from the room were enough to hide his face and although he was wearing the same tunic that his dad was, this man had his tunic open, his chest covered with symbols and markings that Arnold had never seen before.

The man's gaze was firmly fixed upon them, interested in no other in the chamber but them.

"Step forward." His deep, well-spoken voice echoed through the chamber, sending a chill down Arnold's spine. It was a familiar voice and he recognised it. The nature of the voice did not do much to settle Arnold's nerves, which were getting steadily worse. At this point, his legs felt as though they were made of iron, rusted and slow-moving. The trembling was making it hard to walk at all.

Arnold was hesitant, only shuffling forward at a slow pace, in part due to how his legs were feeling but also because the floor ahead of them could not clearly be seen. They steadily moved towards the man who remained stood behind the stone casket, their footsteps echoing through the chamber. They eventually reached him, but the man's face remained hidden in the darkness despite there being nothing but the stone casket between them.

"Redburn, Ethon you are brought here to take part in the ancient Ch'ahb'. You saved the life of a retired member of the Chichen thus have been invited to complete the ceremony that has been passed down for nearly a millennium. Completing this ritual will enable you both to start on your journey of truly mastering your auro, on a path that will enlighten you. It will be a voyage you will be guided through by your spirit beasts. Only once you have completed this voyage will you be able to call yourself Doyen." His words were well-rehearsed, and Arnold fixed his eyes on the shadow laden face.

"Are you ready to proceed?"

"Yes," Otto replied, assured in his response. Arnold felt unsure whether he could go through with it as his nerves were getting the better of him. He wished he could be as calm and cool as Otto was but realising he had come too far to go back, he replied, his voice trembling.

"Yes."

"Then we shall begin," the man replied, his voice sounding even deeper and intimidating than it did before. "You have been approved entry to this Chichen because of the bravery you have shown in combat against someone much stronger than you." The man paused for a short while before continuing, "Without consideration for your own safety, you both stepped into the path of danger to protect another and this is the path that Doyens follow." He stepped back from the stone casket and rubbed a substance across his face. "It is because of this act that you have been approved to enter this ancient Chichen and undertake the Ch'ahb'." Placing his hands in the air, he began to move them in what looked like a circular fashion, whilst humming loudly. His hands began to glow a light green colour, slightly illuminating the area around him. "Doyens are in tune with their auros, enabling them to combine their energy with that of their spirit beasts, more so than anyone that is not a Doyen. Spirit beasts are not only there to guide and protect us when we are in need, but they are also there to protect others. We are connected to our spirit beasts with the very life force that runs through us all. Capture, not kill - that is the way of the Chichen. That is what you must always remember." The man began to chant whilst still moving his hands in a circular motion.

Arnold could not tell what the man was chanting, unable to recognise the language that was being spoken. Remaining focused on the glowing hands, he felt the motion of the hands soothing and felt as though he was falling into a hypnotic trance. Arnold was mesmerised; he was in awe of what he was witnessing.

The man abruptly stopped chanting "The lifeforce that I speak of is your auro, the conduit between your auro and your spirit beast is your blood." Arnold was intrigued by what the man was alluding to. "In order to truly connect your auro to your spirit beast, we need to shed your blood to enable the transition from their world to ours. This is the ancient tradition of the Chichen passed down from the elders to this and all generations." There was a calmness to his voice that Arnold did not expect, given what was being asked of them. Arnold began to be less mesmerised and more concerned. 'Shed blood? What on earth?' he thought.

"That's where the blood-letting comes in then" Otto whispered, distracting Arnold's gaze from the glowing hands in front of him. He felt as though he could no longer see the man stood before him, only what looked like glowing fireflies circling around each other in a smooth motion, as though they were dancing around each other. How could Otto be so calm about this?

"As part of your initiation, you will be required to let your blood spill into the casket before you. This casket is the grave of an ancient elder who once protected this land, his bones consecrated before you. In completing this, you will encourage your spirit beasts to connect with your auro creating a direct line of communication." The man stopped moving his hands and knelt before the casket, his hands still glowing. He leaned forward and picked something up. He stood back up with his arms outstretched, the soft green glow of his hands revealing a blade. He began to move the blade in the air for a few seconds before coming to a stop.

Arnold's heart sank; what on earth was the man going to do to them with that blade? What was his dad going to let the man do to them? Arnold felt conflicted; he trusted his dad, but he did not know this man and had no reason to trust him. His heart was beating faster than ever before, and the adrenaline was pumping through his body. He was beginning to panic, looking around the room for his dad to find some form of reassurance that everything was going to be ok. He couldn't see him anywhere as the darkness engulfed the rest of the room. 'Was this because they had been staring at the light around the man's hands?' he thought to himself. He looked across at Otto who appeared to be completely unfazed about what was happening around them and what was being asked of them. He noticed his dad stood by one of the pillars, illuminated slightly by the flickering flames nearby but mostly hidden within the shadows. He seemed calm and collected, observing everything that was happening, and this helped calm Arnold's nerves a little. 'Dad asked me to trust him, so that's what I need to do,' he reasoned to himself. He was trying his hardest to not show any fear at the situation they faced, and he knew he was failing miserably.

"Hold out your left arm Redburn. Ethon, you hold out your right," the man commanded.

Without hesitation, Otto stretched out his left arm over the top of the stone casket as requested. Arnold wished he could be more like Otto, who was coming across completely calm at this moment whereas he felt like a quivering wreck. He put his right arm forward over the casket, his hand trembling. The more he focused on trying to stop the shaking, the worse it appeared to get.

"Roll back your sleeves," they were instructed, both complying with this request by rolling their sleeve to the top of their arms. "Now, make the connection even stronger by holding hands."

Walking around from behind the casket, the man moved to Otto's side. Drawing the blade level with the top of his arm, he began to project his voice again. "With this blade, I will offer your blood to the spirit gods to enable you to become one with your auro." He pushed the blade against the side of Otto's arm. Arnold saw what was happening and felt instantly queasy, shifting his gaze to straight ahead of him and was just about keeping control of his jellified legs. Otto grimaced, but overall seemed to be in control of the pain he must have been feeling, as he clenched his fist into a tight ball. He looked focused and determined as the man lowered his arm to a 45-degree angle and the blood started to flow, dripping from his clenched fist into the stone casket.

The man then moved from beside Otto and stood by Arnold, pressing the blade against the top of his arm. "With this blade I will offer your blood to the spirit gods to enable you to become one with your auro." Arnold's heart was now racing at a pace he had never experienced; he could hear each heartbeat as if a drum was beating loudly in his ears. He winced as he felt a searing pain in his right arm, gritting his teeth to try not to make a noise but failing as the intense pain forced a cry from his mouth. His arm became crimson as his blood began to make its way down his arm and drip into the casket. Arnold's head began to feel fuzzy and his legs began to feel weak.

"Focus, Arnold." Arthur's voice came from the side of him. He was carrying a flaming torch but interestingly, Arnold noticed the flame on the torch was a light green colour rather than the traditional orange and yellow colour he was accustomed to. Walking straight towards the casket, Arthur lowered the torch into the blood-filled stone grave. The entire casket lit up into green flames, the heat of which Arnold could not feel against his skin which was a strange sensation given how close they both stood to it. If anything, it was soothing. A sense of courage flooded over him and suddenly he felt like he could take on the world, his fears slipping away as the flames danced in front of them.

The flames began to rise into the air above them, swirling around as though the flames were putting on a show for Arnold and Otto. The flames split into two sections and began to swirl around one another and moving in the same circular way that the man had been gesturing with his illuminated hands. The man and Arthur began to chant again in tandem with one another and to Arnold's surprise, the two separate flames began to take shape. To the left and in front of Otto, it formed the shape of a paw with sharp claws. Arnold looked at it, presuming that whatever animal the clawed paw belonged to this would be Otto's spirit beast. Arnold shifted his focus on to the dancing flame that was in front of him. It began to flicker. Arnold waited in anticipation, wondering what form the flame would take, hoping he was about to get a major hint as to the spirit beast he had within him.

The flame flickered again. Otto's flame had not done this - it had formed its shape in a smooth motion. Arnold looked towards his dad who looked equally perplexed as he was. The flame flickered and changed into the form of what looked like a wing, spiked and covered in what looked like scales. Suddenly, it flickered and changed shape again but this time into a wing covered in feathers. The flame then began flickering from the scaled form to the feathered form in quick succession.

"Strange," the man uttered, clearly confused.

"This can't be!" His dad exclaimed. The flames let out a blast which knocked the man and his dad backward, away from the two boys. The flames dropped back into the casket and followed the trail of blood up Arnold and Otto's arms until it reached their cuts that sat at the top. Strangely, Arnold could not feel the heat from the flame crawling up his arm. The sensation was comforting, the throbbing sensation in his arm beginning to subside. After a few seconds the flames extinguished themselves, and as Arnold looked at the top of his arm, he saw that the wound had healed. All that was left was a thin scar where the cut had just been.

"The Ch'ahb' is complete." The man stepped back and walked over to Arthur. "Your connection to your spirit beast has been maximised. Arthur, may I have a word?" Arthur stepped out from the shadows. "Did you see?" asked the man.

"Yes," Arthur replied. "Does this mean what I think it does?" The man nodded.

"It does. It appears that Arnold has a split auro. His spirit beast is still to decide its true form. This is incredibly rare." The man had a concerned expression on his face. "Did you see the forms that the flames took?"

"I did" Arthur replied, his expression equally concerning.

"If that form is what I think it may be, I must inform the Chichen."

"I understand, Sir," Arthur replied, shaking his head in disbelief. Arnold felt like the two of them were talking in riddles and wished they would just talk to him directly rather than around him. Arthur turned and faced Arnold as if he had just heard his thoughts. "How are you both feeling? You did incredibly well." His dad was attempting to divert their attention and Arnold could not believe how nonchalant he suddenly appeared. Otto had a look of wonderment on his face.

"That was amazing!" he exclaimed "You ok, Arnold?" Arnold just stood there, still in shock at what they had just witnessed. He couldn't understand why his arm felt normal despite being cut with the dagger earlier in the process. Even more bizarrely, he could not remember feeling any pain during the ritual, it was as if his memory of the pain had been completely wiped.

"What animals did the flame show?" he asked, desperate to know what his spirit beast was going to be.

"You are on the path to finding this out so we can't tell you. You must discover it for yourself." The man gestured for the two of them to roll down their sleeves. "Now you must research the hieroglyphs that appeared in your Ch'ahb' as this is an indicator of the spirit beast each of you has. You will have access to the literature in the Athenaeum to aid you with this task."

"Why didn't the flames burn?" Otto asked Arthur.

"Because they were not born of this world."

"You mean they are from the-"

"The spirit world, yes," Arthur confirmed. "Boys, follow me back to the changing rooms. Once you have dressed, I will take you to the Athenaeum." Arthur began to walk towards the lift and Arnold and Otto quickly followed. The doors opened instantaneously and the three of them entered. "Was that Mr. Whitaker," Arnold asked, wanting to know who had walked them through the ritual.

"It was, Arnold. Remember he is the Elder, so he runs this Chichen as well as all the others in the North West. It is his job to conduct all the Ch'ahb's in this region." He pressed the button on the lift selecting the ground floor. "Only an Elder can complete the Ch'ahb. Only they have been shown how to access raw energy from the spirit world." The lift doors opened, and his dad escorted them back to the changing rooms.

"Get dressed then come to my office. Can you remember where it is from here?" Arnold nodded and walked into the changing room to get dressed, with Otto following behind. Their bags had been brought across for them from his dad's office. Arnold removed his tunic and walked across to the other side of the room where he could see a large mirror. He turned to the side to examine the scar that was now at the top of his right arm. The scar covered the width of his arm which ran smoothly from one side to the other. His arm still felt a bit numb, but it had begun to feel fuzzy, a sensation similar to pins and needles. Arnold was dumbfounded that his arm had already healed and that he was no longer feeling any pain or any form of discomfort. Otto walked over, also turning to his side to examine his scar.

"That's pretty cool," he said, while he stood appreciating his new-found scar. "This will make us 'edgy' at school you know," he grinned. "What type of spirit beast do you think yours is? I am one hundred percent certain that mine is a big cat. I hope it's a tiger. I can't wait to tell my dad that I am keeping in with family tradition. He will be well chuffed." Arnold began to get himself dressed.

"I think it's safe to say that mine is something that can fly, given the wing that the flame turned into. But there are so many birds out there it would be impossible to guess what it would be." Arnold pulled his t-shirt over his head. "I need to know more about what a split auro means for me."

Otto laughed.

"Trust you not to have a simple auro, it has to be split. No wonder you don't have any signs apart from your super sight." Arnold was a little taken by Otto's comments and about how insensitive they were.

"Glad you find it funny." There was a sharpness to Arnold's voice that was intended to let Otto know that he didn't appreciate his friend's comments. "We can't all have it easy like you, Otto."

"No need to snap," Otto replied, slightly surprised at his friend's reaction to his usual teasing tone.

Arnold continued to get dressed and then left the changing room to go back down to his dad's office without saying another word to Otto. Arnold knew he should not be feeling like this; he should have been on top of the world after finally seeing inside a Chichen and completing his initiation ritual. Instead, he felt deflated at what he perceived to be another setback. "Why for once could it not be straight forward for me?" he muttered to himself "Why is it me that has to have a split auro?"

Nothing positive ever seemed to happen concerning his spirit beast. He had a split auro, his grandad knew something about his spirit beast, but he didn't know where he was to talk to him - he felt like he'd had enough. He genuinely felt that for every step forward he made, life was pushing him backwards three steps. The way he was feeling, he just wanted to go home and climb into bed. Arnold felt that if he was to research anything around his spirit beast today, whatever he found he would only find himself further disappointed.

As he shuffled down the corridor contemplating simply walking past his dad's office and going straight home. He decided against this and made his way into his dad's office, pushing the door open in a manner to try and alert his dad that he wasn't happy.

"Woah there - what's wrong with you?" his dad asked. "Where's Otto?"

"He's finishing getting dressed. He shouldn't be long. What's a split auro?" Arnold wanted to know what his dad and Mr. Whitaker meant by the phrase and his tone of voice indicated that he didn't want to be fobbed off. His dad was sat at his desk and dressed in the clothes he was wearing before he had put his tunic on. He shut his laptop and leaned forward placing his arms on his desk. "Calm down and sit down." His dad was assertive and direct. Arnold didn't move. "Sit there, son and I will explain."

"I'll stay standing thanks." Arnold didn't have a reason to be off with his dad, but he was just in a bad mood now.

"There is no need to be like that. Remember that I am your dad first before anything else. I wouldn't accept you talking to me like that at home and I certainly will not accept it here." There was a tone to his voice that Arnold recognised as the one you didn't ignore. He walked over to the chair at the opposite side of the desk and sat down looking sheepish.

The office door swung open and Otto walked in, pulling the chair out next to Arnold. He gave Arnold a disapproving look before sitting next to him, clearly not happy with the way he had just spoken to him in the changing rooms. Arthur looked at the two of them, sensing the atmosphere, and he began to answer Arnold's first question. "Split auros are rare, and to put it frankly, neither myself nor Mr. Whitaker have come across one before. When an auro is split it means that your spirit best is undecided on its form. It means that it is unsure on the path it needs to guide you on."

"That doesn't sound complicated," Otto replied. "Even I can understand that."

"It is more getting your head around the concept." Arthur continued. "A split auro means that your spirit beast doesn't know how best to guide you in times of need, whether that be through wisdom, courage, strength, cunning-"

"How do you know that?" Arnold interrupted, not fully understanding what his dad was meaning.

A concerned expression came over his dad's face.

"During the Ch'ahb', your flame flickered between two forms. It is difficult to ascertain what your spirit beast could be as one form suggested a bird-like creature." His dad paused clearly uncomfortable at the discussion they were having. Arnold pressed his dad, wanting to know exactly what he was alluding to. "And the other?" His dad sighed.

"The other form the flame took was clearly a representation of the dragon spirit beast. This is a darker path; aggression and cunning are just two of the traits common to this type of spirit beast as well as unforgiving anger. There has not been anyone with a known dragon spirit beast for a long time." His dad's gaze appeared to become hazy whilst explaining this.

Arnold's heart began to race. This was what he had heard his dad and grandad talking about just a few nights ago. So, this what his dad was concerned about; that he was showing signs of a dragon spirit beast and he was going to walk down a darker path. Did this mean that he was going to be a bad person?

"Hang on, I thought you weren't allowed to tell us what the flames indicated?" Otto asked before Arnold had a chance to.

"Sometimes you need to go against tradition. A dragon spirit beast is not good news and I intend to make sure that you do not go down that path, Arnold. It doesn't even bear thinking about." His dad's voice broke slightly, making him appear more vulnerable than Arnold had ever seen him before. "I will be in a deep grave before I ever see my son walk down that path. I will not let something like that take you, son; a dragon spirit beast is uncontrollable."

"I do get a say in this, dad. I'm not interested in being bad so even if I went down that path it doesn't necessarily mean disaster." Arnold was confused as to why his integrity was being questioned as if they did not already know that he was a good person.

"You don't understand, Arnold. For your auro to be split, it means that your spirit beast is unsure of the direction you would go when faced with difficult decisions."

"Oh," Arnold replied, starting to feel like he was a bad person even though he hadn't actually done anything.

"It's been a long evening so let's leave the Athenaeum to tomorrow. You have both had a lot to take in." His dad began to pack up the things that were on his desk. "Come on, I'll drop you off too, Otto."

Arnold felt even more deflated than before. It was like he'd felt earlier; the more he found out, the worse everything seemed to get. Three steps back. And now his spirit beast might be a dragon, and everyone was panicking. Suddenly, out of nowhere, Arnold had a thought. *What if they were wrong? What if a dragon spirit beast could be a good thing? What if he could control it?* These thoughts circled around in his head as he left the Chichen.

Chapter Ten

Arnold had not been the most motivated person in Oswald today. He had spent the whole day feeling lethargic and uninterested in everything. All he'd wanted all his life was to be a Doyen and train in the Chichen like his dad had and as his grandad had before him. He had been given this fantastic opportunity and he felt that the experience was ruined by learning he had a split auro.

He hadn't spoken a word to his parents that morning and had left for school before Otto had the chance to arrive. Otto was just at the bottom of his street as Arnold left his house. He paused for a few seconds, undecided if he was going to wait for his friend or just carry on with his walk to school by himself. He didn't know whether he was genuinely mad at Otto or just venting his frustration stemming from the Ch'ahb' at him. In the end, he stopped to allow his friend time to catch him up. Otto had sped up and easily caught up to Arnold. He had a grin that spanned ear to ear having had a much better experience of the Ch'ahb' than Arnold had.

"Morning, mate. I would ask how you are feeling but the fact that your face is matching the weather tells me everything." It was a wet morning and though it wasn't raining now it had been all night. A layer of fog sat on the streets, with the skies above looking particularly grey. He was not wrong; Arnold was in a foul mood.

The two of them continued their regular journey and soon enough they were at the gates to the school. Something felt different today, though. As the two of them entered school it felt like the other students were whispering and looking at the two of them as they walked by. Arnold felt his cheeks begin to glow as he began blushing right on cue, a sense of paranoia overcoming him.

"Have we got our clothes on back to front or something?" Otto barked bullishly at one pupil who was pointing the two of them out to their circle of friends. The pupil quickly turned their attention back to the friends and avoided eye contact with Otto. "It's rude to point," he muttered to Arnold as they continued to their form rooms.

Nothing changed though as the two of them made their way through the network of hallways. Everyone was whispering to each other, some smiling at them, some looking nervously towards them as though they had three heads.

"What is going on with everyone?" Otto asked out loud.

"They must know about the Chichen but how though? Did you tell anyone?" Arnold asked.

"Not that I remember. Only Everett and George know." Arnold wanted the ground to open up and swallow him. He hated being the centre of attention, unlike Otto who didn't seem to be too bothered about everyone looking, whispering and talking about them. He was more interested in exactly what the gossip was. Arnold was more concerned that they somehow knew about his split auro.

At the bottom of the hallway, they could see Everett and George stood talking, Everett appearing to be giving George a scolding. Arnold and Otto headed over to speak to them thinking that they would want to know how the previous night had gone, even though Arnold didn't feel particularly keen on explaining his split auro. As they reached the pair, Everett looked mad and it didn't take a genius to realise who she was mad at. George's body language told the story as she stood there with her head down unable to look either Arnold or Otto in the eye.

"What's happening here?" Otto dived straight in, unable to subtly ask leading questions. Everett stood with her arms folded. "George has something she wants to tell you." George continued to look at the ground and began nervously moving her foot around on the floor.

"I'm sorry," she said, quietly. Arnold was confused as he had no idea why George would be apologising to them. Everything had been fine yesterday after school. She looked up at the two of them only managing intermittent eye contact before looking down at the floor once more. "I was talking to Everett about you two joining the Chichen on our way home from school." Her tone of voice changed as she spoke, indicating that she felt bad about something. "Well you know, we know about the Chichen because we were invited too. I didn't realise, well you see..."

"George!" Everett interjected, scolding her again and prompting her to not to go off on a tangent.

"Sorry, as I was saying-"

"Dawdling," Everett corrected.

George looked at Everett and continued, "I was talking to Everett while we were walking home and I didn't realise that Peter Yarwood was behind me, along with Dan and Gary". She looked down at the floor again. "They heard me, and I think it is clear to see that they have told everybody about you two and the Chichen." Arnold felt relieved that there wasn't an untrue rumour going around again like in year seven. That situation had been a nightmare for Arnold and he had seriously considered switching schools.

"We're cool," Otto said, grinning and puffing his chest out, happy at everyone knowing about the Chichen.

"No one else is meant to know," Arnold reminded him, feeling increasingly worried. "We are really young to be allowed to join. Do you want to be the one who accidentally tells people about the secrets of the Chichen, because I don't want to be that person!"

"Well if it isn't Arnold and Otto," a voice shouted from behind them. Arnold turned to see Peter stood there with Dan and Gary at either side of him. "Anything you boys want to tell us?" The boy was the very personification of arrogance with his athletic build, wavy blonde hair and sneering expression. Dan stood to his left, his head shaven, three stud earrings in his left ear. Arnold had heard that Dan had a tattoo, but he had never seen it. To Peter's right stood Gary. He was taller than Peter and was also athletically built, his mop of curly hair parting around his dark eyes.

"I took your mum out on a date last night. No hard feelings, Pete." Otto fired back sarcastically. "Your mum's next, Dan. You don't mind, do you?"

"Funny," Peter responded, unimpressed. Dan looked considerably more unhappy, his scowl showing his frustration at being mocked. Peter walked over and wrapped his arm around Arnold trying to coax information out of him. "I heard you two somehow got invited to the Chichen. Didn't realise they let menials in." Arnold had never really spoken with Peter before and found it strange that he was suddenly interested in them.

"Not really, I've nothing to say," Arnold said, choosing to keep tight-lipped and ignore the taunt.

"Don't be like that Arnold. We are all friends, here." There was a smarmy tone to Peter's voice; he was arrogant and popular, a real firestorm of a combination at school.

"Leave him alone," Everett said.

'No Everett, you're only going to make things worse,' Arnold thought. Peter removed his arm from around Arnold and turned to face Everett. "Boar off," he sneered. Peter looked back at Dan and Gary and the three of them began sniggering at Everett's expense. Arnold didn't know what to do but before thinking, he had already spoken.

"Don't talk to her like that." Arnold's heart immediately sank, realising what he had just done. He was a lot less confident than he had sounded. Peter turned around, unimpressed at Arnold.

"Who do you think you're talking to?" The thick Scottish accent from Gary was every bit intimidating as it was intended. Gary and Dan walked up to Arnold and began to push him about between each other.

"Did you say something?" Dan sniggered as he shoved Arnold back towards Gary.

"I didn't mean anything," Arnold said quietly, not really knowing what to do. He had never got into trouble before and he had certainly never had a fight. Arnold looked at the floor not wanting to make eye contact with either of them.

"Didn't think you said anything." Peter laughed. "And you've been accepted in the Chichen? That lot are really letting their standards drop." With that, Peter pushed Arnold with force. Losing his footing, Arnold fell back into the wall behind him before falling to the floor.

"Peter, stop it!" cried Everett.

"Or?" he asked, his cockiness oozing out of him. Peter suddenly found himself pushed up against the wall by Otto, who had lunged at him. Otto grabbed hold of Peter by the scruff off his shirt collar "Keep your hands off him," he growled, not intimidated by Peter or his oafish friends. Everett, seeing the change in mood, dropped her bag from her shoulder into her hand and swung for Dan, crashing it against his side. Gary ran up behind Otto and wrapped his arms around him, locking him in a bear hug. Otto pushed back from Peter with as much force as he could, pushing Gary, who lost his balance and fell onto his back with Otto landing on top of him. Dan had stepped in and grabbed hold of Otto to pick him up from the floor but suddenly found himself on the floor next to Otto and Gary as Everett had barged into him, pushing him over. Peter straightened up his tie from where Otto had grabbed him and looked at Arnold in disgust as he sat on the floor, frozen in the situation and unaware of how to respond.

"Come on, get up you two. They're not worth it." He helped Gary up first before assisting Dan with getting to his feet. "See you around Arnold." He shoved Arnold in the shoulder, knocking him back against the wall.

"Soon," Gary added.

"And next time, your boyfriend and girlfriend won't be here to protect you," Dan finished as the three of them walked down the corridor.

Arnold felt so embarrassed by what had just happened. Why couldn't he be that bit more confident like Otto was? Arnold gathered himself and climbed to his feet, ashamed of himself for not putting up a better fight and hoping that no one else had seen what had happened. His fears were realised, however, as lots of other pupils had seen the commotion and the halls were buzzing with the scuffle that had just taken place. Everett stood over Otto and helped him to his feet.

"You ok?" she asked, dusting his blazer down to straighten it up for him. "You held your own, there."

"Meh," he replied. "Arnold would have done the same for me. You mess with one of us, you mess with both of us."

"All of us," Everett added. Arnold couldn't help but notice the admiration that Everett had in her eyes as she cast a fixed gaze at Otto, and he felt another wave of jealousy come over him. He felt he had no chance with Everett if her attention were to turn towards his friend. "Thanks for sticking up for me, too." Everett temporarily took her eyes from Otto as she spoke to Arnold.

"You stuck up for me first," Arnold replied. 'Today couldn't have started any worse,' he thought to himself. It wasn't nine o'clock yet and he already felt like going home. "Thanks for helping me," he said to Otto, grateful for his assistance annoyed at himself for feeling jealous of how Otto had handled the situation better than he had. The bell rang indicating that they had five minutes to get to their form rooms so the four of them went their separate ways and headed to register for the day.

Arnold spent the rest of the day keeping himself to himself, avoiding all his peers and choosing to spend the breaks in solitude within the school library. He was already tired of people gawping at him. By the end of the day, Arnold didn't feel like going to the Chichen and this was only day two since completing the Ch'ahb'. He so wished that he felt more motivated than he did, but he knew that he needed to just get his head down and get on with the training. Surely it would only be a matter of time before something positive happened.

Arnold left his final class of the day and headed to the front of the school to wait for Otto. To his surprise, he was already waiting for him which was very uncharacteristic.

"In a rush?" Arnold felt able to muster some sarcastic humour despite his mood.

"Excited to learn more. Last night was the best experience I have ever had!" His enthusiasm was written all over his face. "I want to get stuck into the work that we have been set and find out what our spirit beasts are going to be." He paused for a moment noticing that Arnold was nowhere near as excited as he was. "I know you're annoyed about yesterday but let's just give it a try and see how we get on in the Chichen tonight." Arnold admired Otto's enthusiasm and really appreciated him trying to encourage him. For his own sanity, Arnold decided that he would not ruin the evening by being moody.

"I'll try and be more positive," he pledged.

The two set off to the Chichen and after around five minutes they reached the stone steps that sat just before the large oak entrance to the building. The two walked through the front door and were greeted by Sue.

"Good evening, boys. How are you both today?" Her smile was infectious and instantly made Arnold feel welcome and he felt that some of his apprehension and anxiety had lifted.

"How do we get to the Athenaeum?" Otto asked, his eagerness getting in the way of his manners. Not that he normally had them; Otto wasn't exactly known for them and was oblivious at times to how rude he could seem.

"Hi," Arnold said, speaking on behalf of them both. "Could you please tell us where the Athenaeum is? Mr. Whitaker has set us a task to complete." He wondered where his dad might be as he spoke with Sue, thinking that he would have been there to greet the two of them.

"You mean the Athe-nae-um," Sue corrected, breaking the words down into three sections to explain how the word was pronounced. "Sorry, you were pronouncing it wrong. It's the Ath-e-nae-um." She broke it down into four parts to try and make it easier for Otto to understand. Arnold felt glad that she had done that as he would have been unable to repeat what she had said. Sue pointed her hand to the side of her desk. "If you follow the hallway here you can't miss it but you will both need to register your fingerprints with me first so I can grant you access." She waved the two of them over to her desk. The two of them obliged and walked across the reception area and stood in front of Sue's desk. "You first Arnold. Please just put your index finger on the pressure pad in front of you until I say." She tapped her hand on the small device that was fixed into the desk. The glass covering it was a dark red colour and Arnold could see the many fingerprints from other people who had been registered before them. Arnold placed his index finger as directed by Sue on the small device and after a short while the device let out a short beep. "You can take your finger off, now. Otto please can you do the same?" Otto placed his finger on the device and again a short beep sounded, indicating that Sue had registered his fingerprint." Mr. Whitaker has given you access to the Athenaeum for now. This is the only area of the Chichen where you have access to until you are told otherwise by Mr. Whitaker." Sue spoke with efficiency as though the three of them were in a business meeting. "Until then, this is the only area you are permitted to enter on your own." She pointed down the hallway again. "The Athenaeum is down the hallway. When you get there, place your finger against the device by the door and this will grant you access." Sue smiled at them both and then looked back down at her desk and began to write in the diary that was next to the phone.

Arnold could not contain his excitement; they were about to begin their first task since joining the Chichen. He could only hope that by the end of today he would be that little bit closer to finding out what his spirit beast was going to be.

"And you're back in the room!" Otto caught Arnold's attention by snapping his fingers in front of his face. Arnold had found himself in a daydream thinking about his split auro.

A dragon or a bird.

Chapter Eleven

Arnold and Otto made their way down the hallway until they reached large, frosted double doors. As Sue had told them, to the right of the door was the same type of device as at the front desk where they had registered their fingerprints. Otto put his hand out and placed his index finger on the red glass in the centre of the device. After a few seconds, the familiar bleep from the device sounded and the frosting from the glass vanished in an instant. A few seconds later, the doors slid open granting the two of them access. Arnold stepped through the door and was immediately struck by the money that must have gone into creating this room. There were multiple rows of bookshelves running the length of the room, with books running from floor to ceiling from one edge of the wall to the next. In the centre of the room stood a screen fixed to a table.

"Woah." Arnold gasped as he looked around the room, impressed with the layout. This was like no library he had ever seen before. Otto had already made his way to the glowing screen in the centre of the room. Arnold loved reading books, but Otto was the complete opposite. and much preferred to use technology to improve his knowledge. While he looked at the computer screen, Arnold gazed around the room, trying to take in all the detail. From the intricately tiled floor to the impressive carvings that covered the bookshelves, the library was a sight to behold.

"This makes it miles easier," Otto said, motioning for Arnold to come and look at the screen with him. Arnold walked across to see what he was talking about. "Looks like you can type in what you are looking for and it will tell us where to look. This will be simple." There was a smugness in Otto's tone. He sat down in the chair in front of the screen and cracked his knuckles, somewhat over dramatically. He then typed in 'big cats' and immediately the screen let out a loud noise to indicate that the search had been denied. Arnold laughed at Otto's surprise, having already figured out that it would not have been that easy.

"Looks like it's blocked."

"What now?" Otto asked, seeking advice from Arnold.

"We're doing this the old-fashioned way," he replied, looking at the vast expanse of books within the room and feeling just a bit daunted. Arnold realised that they would have to figure out how the books were organised; he knew he wanted to find anything on spirit beasts that could fly but did not have a clue where to start.

"Bugger." Otto sighed. He wasn't as patient as Arnold.

"Best dive in.," Arnold said, knowing that this was going to take some time to find what they were looking for. Arnold walked to the first row of books and began looking at the first shelf to see what order the books were in. However, he could not figure it out. They were not in alphabetical order, author order, size order, topic order or indeed any logical order and he felt incredibly confused.

"Sack this!" Otto shouted. "Someone has mixed all these up. It doesn't make any sense!" He carried on staring at the wall of books, not knowing where to start.

"We're going to have to look at these books one at a time until we find something that means something to us." Arnold felt more upbeat than Otto even though he knew that this was going to take some time to achieve. He began to pull out the books from the shelf in no particular order. He picked a book out which was on the history of

Oswald which he promptly put back on to the shelf. 'This is going to take forever,' Arnold thought to himself. Looking across at Otto, he couldn't help but laugh out loud at the sight of him looking utterly bemused at the enormous number of books that stood before him. With his hands on his hips looking up at the books, Otto looked like he was being proactive but actually, he was overwhelmed and didn't really know what to do next. Arnold began to walk slowly down the aisle, choosing to focus on the top shelf of books. He walked slowly, reading the titles of each book as he walked past. Once he had got to the bottom of the first aisle, he began to walk back to his starting point, this time focusing on the next shelf down. After around twenty minutes of this process, Arnold called across to Otto who was now stood further up the opposite side of the Athenaeum, still staring.

"I think it's safe to say this first row of books is about history," Arnold announced. "Have you found anything interesting yet?"

"No. I haven't got a clue what I am looking at here. Doesn't seem to be anything on big cat spirit beasts." He paused. "Oh hang on, think I might have something up there." Otto looked confused as he looked around the room.

"What's wrong?"

"How am I meant to get it down? There are no ladders in here." Otto seemed frustrated at the lack of tools available for them to complete their tasks. "Don't let me forget that book is up there, and I'll come back to it, later." Arnold smiled to himself. At least Otto was engaged in trying to find books despite it being something he wouldn't normally be vaguely interested in.

Arnold and Otto spent their entire evening after school in the Athenaeum, trying their hardest to find specific books about groups and types of spirit animals. However, so far, they hadn't found one. Arnold had found the process quite therapeutic and had got into a steady routine, making his way through the vast archive of books that filled the room. Otto, on the other hand, was stressed.

"This is like being in prison!" Otto cried. "This is so unhelpful."

"You are not being forced to be here," Arnold said, checking yet another book for a relevant title.

"I know that I'm just saying." In truth, throughout the evening, the two of them had managed to check every row of books and up to now, there was nothing they could see that they felt would be any use to them.

"Right, I've had enough." An inpatient Otto had begun pacing the large wall of books on the far side of the Athenaeum. "I'm getting that book up there." Otto pointed at the book he was certain would contain information on big cats, even though it was too high up for him to work out the title. "Can you use your super eyes and see up there?"

Arnold focused on the direction that Otto was pointing and he was pleased to clearly see the names of the books on the high shelf. He glanced around the section that Otto was pointing out, realising that he had been right all along. There was a book there that looked like it could be about big cats. It read 'Spirit Beasts of Africa'. Looking at the books just above it, Arnold realised that it was the upper section of the wall that contained the books that they were looking for. Otto had been right with his hunch earlier on and Arnold kicked himself at the time they had wasted looking at the other sections of the Athenaeum. "You're right," Arnold informed him. "Now, how do we get to them down?" He looked around the room but apart from solid wood carved bookshelves, there was no sign of anything that the two of them could use to scale the wall of books and reach the section they needed.

"Come here!" Otto shouted. "I've got an idea. Stand by that wall." Arnold did as he was asked and walked towards the corner of the room and looked at Otto for further instructions.

"I'm going to face the wall." Not sounding too confident in his idea he continued anyway, "and you need to climb up on my shoulders...then I will walk across the wall to where the book is, and you grab it. You can use the window ledge there to pull yourself up onto my shoulders." Arnold felt that the theory was full of holes, but Otto had the athletic build now to be able to carry his weight. The only question he had was, would he be able to move around with him up there? Otto got himself into position and crouched down on the floor to give Arnold a lower area to climb, using the window ledge next to them to balance. Arnold placed one foot on to Otto's shoulder and pushed himself up from the ground. As his momentum took him upwards, he placed his other foot on Otto's other shoulder and grabbed hold of the window ledge to stop him from falling off. "That wasn't too bad was it?" Otto grinned. "Ok, now keep your balance." He began to slowly push himself from the ground to a standing position. It was a good job it was Otto underneath as Arnold would not have been able to do this. Otto kept his hands against the wall in front of him to keep his balance and Arnold shifted his hands from the window ledge to the face of the wall. A sense of panic washed over him and Arnold felt very vulnerable as he had nothing to hold on to. Otto managed to get his legs fully extended and began to step slowly sideways until eventually the pair of them became level with the relevant wall of books. Otto was concentrating and his legs were just threatening to buckle. Putting his hands in a position to balance against the shelves and the books, Arnold started reading the spines of the books to find the one that Otto wanted. He couldn't see the book at first but then realised that they were still not tall enough, as the book remained just out of his reach.

"I can't reach it," he gasped, attempting to slowly reach out his hand in another attempt to grab the book. "I'm still not high enough."

"Ok, hang on." Otto shuffled his feet and tried to stand on his tiptoes, to try to lift Arnold up higher. He let out a grunt as the strain from Arnold standing on him began to set in. Keeping his arm outstretched, Arnold could just reach the bottom of the book but not enough for him to grab it. Arnold began to lower as Otto needed to secure his feet, the strenuous task beginning to tire him.

"I can't keep you there much longer, you're going to have to hurry up," he groaned. "I think I've got one more try in me. Hold on." Otto began to push up on to his toes again and pushed up his shoulders to get Arnold up as high as possible. Arnold reached for the book again but was still too far away. He looked and pulled out the two books next to it and dropped them behind him. The book he wanted then fell towards him into the gap he had created, meaning he was able to grab hold of it. Arnold then saw a book beyond it that read 'Dragon's, Birds and Dreams'. That was too much of a coincidence.

"Hang on there's another book here that I need," he said, stretching as far as he could.

"Hurry up." Arnold reached out but lost his footing, his foot sliding from Otto's shoulders. Propelling himself forward, he grabbed at the book he needed, part wanting the book and part trying to grab hold of anything to stop him falling. He failed miserably at both. He fell sideways, taking out multiple shelves of books as he fell to the floor. He heard a crunching noise as he slammed to the floor realising it was Otto underneath him, as he had taken him down, too. There was an almighty crash as an avalanche of books began to fall from the wall and land on top of them, each corner of a book that landed on them causing further discomfort. When the books eventually stopped falling, the two of them let out a loud groan at what had just happened to them. Arnold frowned as he realised the trouble they were about to be in.

"My dad is going to kill me."

"Never mind that - Mr. Whitaker is going to go mental. Did you get the book I needed, and can you please get off me?" a muffled voice said from underneath Arnold.

Pushing the books away and rolling to his side before climbing back to his feet Arnold turned and leaned over to help Otto free himself from the books. The two of them stood there, looking at the pile of books on the floor. Otto winced at the empty bookshelves and then shrugged. "Job done, that will make it easier for us," he stated, as he knelt and picked up the book that he had asked Arnold to grab. "I'll be over there with this," he said, walking off to a desk and leaving Arnold staring at the pile of books on the floor before him. Arnold hoped that the book he wanted was within the pile so he dropped to his knees and began removing the books, one at a time. The task became more laborious with every book that he removed from the pile and Arnold felt like giving up on finding the book that he so desperately needed. He removed some more books and was relieved to finally find the book he was looking for. He picked it up from the pile, a rare smile finding its way to his face. Finally. Something positive.

Grasping the 'Dragons, Birds and Dreams' book he stared at the cover and felt like he was holding some of the answers that he needed. As he stood there, something caught his eye in the pile of books that lay on the ground. To the side of a pile lay an open book, with a picture on one of the pages that looked instantly familiar to him. Putting the book in his hands to one side, he walked over to take a closer look at the book on the floor, bending down to pick it up and examine it closer. On the page was a drawing of a dagger that had intricate inscriptions within the blade and the handle. A chill ran through him; he had seen this dagger before. It was from the evening of Arnold's birthday when they saved the old Doyen. The scarred man had this blade and Arnold knew it. He'd seen it too up close and personal not to know it. The black hilt was described as being made of ebony and the blade itself had been created from rare ivory taken from an elephant spirit beast. Arnold stared at the picture for a minute or so taking in every detail he could, from the carvings to the peculiar shape of the handle and the blade. He turned the book over to check the title. It read 'Ancient Artefacts of the Spirit Realm' and it was by an author called Betsy Devon whom Arnold had never heard of before.

"Otto, come here - you need to see this." Otto came over straight away, hearing the urgency in Arnold's voice.

"What?"

"Look at this." Arnold showed him the page with the drawing of the dagger and Otto glanced back at him, not understanding what he was saying.

"He had this blade that night, the scarred man has this dagger." Arnold was absolutely sure there was no mistaking it.

"I didn't see it, are you sure?"

"Definitely." Arnold replied, never more certain of anything in his life.

"Does it say anything about it?" Otto quizzed, pressing Arnold to read more. He read the wording on the opposite page of the drawing which read 'The Blade of the Spirits.' He turned the page to see if there were any more information on the blade and there was. Arnold began to recite the paragraph which read;

"13th April 1951

This investigation had proved nothing but troublesome from start to finish. After spending eleven months searching for the blade of the spirits, we had all but given up. That was until we received a new lead. A month after we had received this lead and following the directions, we were given we eventually found the ancient ruins of the temple. We entered the temple with high hopes of finally securing this ancient artefact and to our joy, it was there on an overgrown pedestal. We are in the process of translating the hieroglyphs which denote two giant mane-less lions. Could it be that this blade is the one that controls 'The Lions of Tsavo'? If our findings are correct, then somehow the two giant spirit beasts can be controlled by whoever holds the blade. There are more hieroglyphs left to translate about which we are eagerly awaiting feedback.

This is the blade that we need for the ceremony.

This is the blade we need to save my best friend.

Betsy Devon"

Arnold turned to the next page to see pictures of the hieroglyphs that Betsy Devon had spoken about and true to her word, they resembled ancient carvings that denoted two mane-less lions. He re-read the paragraph wanting to take in as much information as possible and then passed the book to Otto so that he could read the pages.

Otto scratched his head bemused at what he was reading. "What are the Lions of Tsavo?"

"I don't know but I want to find out." Feeling re-motivated, Arnold made for the door to speak with his dad about what they had discovered.

"And where do you think you are going?" Mr. Whitaker stood at the doorway of the Athenaeum, unimpressed at the mess before him.

"We need to speak to-"

"No." Mr. Whitaker cut Arnold off mid-sentence. "What you need to do is leave this room in the condition that you found it." He walked over to the screen that was in the centre of the room and began to press the keypad. Next to the double doors, a cupboard opened that neither had noticed and within it a set of ladders. "Use these to put the books you don't need back where you found them. Then you can go and speak to your dad." He turned on his heel and walked out of the room, the double doors sliding shut behind him.

"As if the ladders were there all along! That's so annoying," Otto groaned.

"Yeah, but we wouldn't have found this if we'd used them."

Arnold clutched the book with the drawings of the dagger to his chest. He knew that so many questions were about to be answered and he couldn't wait.

Chapter Twelve

It took Arnold and Otto around two hours to put all the books back in place in the Athenaeum and they were both starting to flag. Otto let out a huge yawn, signaling his tiredness and readiness to go home. "This has taken forever. Mr. Whitaker seemed completely different from the Ch'ahb', didn't he?" Otto was referencing the stern tone that Mr. Whitaker had taken with them earlier when he had seen the devastation they had caused. "No need to be like that with us," he sulked, still unimpressed at the way they were spoken to.

"To be fair we had just trashed the Athenaeum, even if it was an accident," Arnold said. "I just want to finish up here so we can go and see my dad. I need to tell him about the dagger because it might help find the scarred man." Arnold was sure the dagger the scarred man had was the same as the one he had seen in the book. He climbed the ladder, balancing three more books. Just over halfway up, Arnold stopped to place the books back on the shelf. He was past the point of caring if the books were in order, he just wanted to leave the Athenaeum and ask his dad some questions. "Right, I think that's it," he sighed as he climbed back down the ladders, relieved at finally completing the arduous task. He stepped off the bottom rung of the ladder and made his way to the large glass double doors at the entrance, picking up the book titled 'Ancient Artefacts of the Spirit Realm'. He looked back at Otto. "Have you got your book?" Otto nodded and followed Arnold to the exit.

They exited the room with the glass doors frosting up as soon as they shut behind them and made their way down the hallway and back to the reception area. Sue was just finishing for the day as she switched off her computer and stood up to put on her long, light pink coat, "Have you boys all finished? I'm not going to lie - you were both very entertaining on the CCTV." She chuckled to herself as she picked up her bag and placed it over her shoulder. "If you are looking for your dad, he is in his office waiting to take you both home. I will see you both on Monday." She walked from behind the desk and exited the building, waving to them as she walked through the doors.

Arnold and Otto headed to his dad's office, remembering their way from the first time they had arrived at the Chichen. They knocked on the door and waited for a response.

"Come in." Arnold pushed the door open and made his way in. "I've found something, Dad." Not wanting to waste any time he got straight to the point.

"About your spirit beast?" he asked.

"It's about the scarred man," Otto added.

"The scarred man? How?" Arnold walked over to his dad's desk and placed the book they had stumbled upon, opening it to the page with the drawing of the dagger. His dad studied the picture for a short while before lifting his head to look at Arnold, wanting him to explain why he was looking at this picture.

"What is this?"

"It's the blade that I saw that night, this was the blade that the scarred man had," Arnold told him excitedly.

"Are you sure?" his dad asked, frowning. "Let me see that." He grabbed at the book and flicked through the journal that Arnold had found. "In this book, it's only a drawing."

"I'm sure dad, that's the blade that the scarred man was carrying."

"If this is true, then he has an extremely dangerous artefact."

"I'm a hundred percent certain dad, I know what I saw. I saw this blade in his hands." Arnold turned the pages over to the paragraph he had read. "What are the Lions of Tsavo?"

"The Lions of Tsavo?" Arthur repeated.

"Yes. Read that paragraph - Betsy Devon mentions them." Arnold again pointed at the paragraph that was written about trying to find the dagger.

"It's a true story. Well, part of it is. You see, there are many myths about the Lions of Tsavo however none were ever found to be true," his dad explained to them. Arnold and Otto sat down on the chairs opposite his dad's desk, both completely drawn into the conversation and both equally fascinated by what they were being told. Arthur began to go into detail about what he knew. "The Tsavo lions are two man-hunting lions that were meant to have terrorised workers who were building a new railway line in the Tsavo region of Africa, in the late eighteen hundreds. There were significant differences to normal lions as these lions were larger than usual, more powerful and even though they were male they did not have a mane." His dad interlocked his hands as he began to explain the history behind the myth.

"That's pretty cool." Otto was entranced at the tale they were being told.

Arnold's dad continued "It wasn't cool, at the time this was terrifying for the workers. Between March and December, it was estimated that they had killed over a hundred workers on the railway line. These lions were clever and did not fall for any traps that were set to capture them. Also, they stalked their prey like they knew who they wanted to kill. They were eventually hunted and killed by John Patterson who was one of the lead engineers of the railway line." Arthur leaned further forward. "Now what was interesting was that the lion's target appeared to be Patterson. Every camp he visited, workers would go missing to the point where at one time, locals began to suspect him as having some form of control over the lions," Arthur said, concluding his tale.

"And the theory?" Arnold pressed his dad, desperately wanting to know the rest of the story.

"There was a story amongst the workers that the lions were under the control of a shaman who used a dagger that he had enchanted. Not happy with the railway line being built, he wanted to stop it from progressing by targeting Patterson. After the Lions were killed, it was said that the Shaman took the spirits of these animals and transferred them to a blade where they were to be kept, granting whoever held it the ability to summon them." Arthur leaned back in his chair.

"Like a spirit beast?" Arnold asked.

"Yes. No one knows where the dagger went after that, however, so it is seen as a myth, an old story."

"Until now, that is. I mean, if the scarred man has the dagger-" Otto began.

"He does." Arnold finished, knowing that he was not mistaken that this was the same dagger that he had seen. Arnold's dad appeared more sceptical than Arnold and Otto and stood up from behind his desk. "We need more evidence. Mr. Whitaker will not proceed on a hunch."

"But Dad, I know what I saw!"

"Sorry Arnold, we need more proof before we can do anything. I'm not saying I do not believe you, but I know how Mr. Whitaker works and he will want some evidence." His dad began to tidy his desk. "Come on, boys. It's getting late now, let's head home." Arnold felt the frustration building in him again, wishing that his dad would just take his word. It seemed that it didn't matter what he did or said, his dad would always find some way of casting doubt over what he was doing or in this case of his theory of the dagger.

Feeling dejected, Arnold withdrew into himself, choosing to not engage in any further conversation. He picked his schoolbag up from the floor and placed the old book inside it knowing he would spend the rest of the night reading as much of it as possible.

"You ok?" Otto asked, knowing that Arnold wouldn't be happy at his dad not taking his word about the dagger.

"I'll be fine. Getting used to it, now." He placed his bag on his shoulder and began to follow his dad down to the car park. The three of them got in the car and Arnold's dad set off towards Otto's house to drop him off first. An awkward silence filled the vehicle as Arnold sat in the front seat, choosing to stare out the window to avoid looking at his dad. The story of the Lions of Tsavo ran through his head and he began to wonder that, if true, how a dagger could control the two beasts and if a shaman really had been involved. Was it even possible to create such a powerful artefact? Arnold had read that Shamans could create artefacts, but he didn't know if they existed anymore. It was a practice that was unheard of these days because of how rare it was for someone to be able to connect to the spirit world in the way that they could, never mind be able to harness their energy and transfer it to items of their choosing. In the old days this was in the form of weapons and trinkets, so the dagger theory was starting to sound a pretty safe one.

Before long the car pulled up outside Otto's house, and he climbed out. "Thanks," he said, before shutting the car door and heading to his house. Arnold nodded towards him and his dad waved from behind the steering wheel, setting off driving again as Otto shut his front door behind him. The awkward silence continued within the car with Arnold to continue to stare out of the window. It was Arthur who broke the silence first.

"I didn't say I didn't believe you, I just said we needed more evidence to back up what you were saying," Arthur explained, attempting to reassure Arnold and bring him back around. "You can't fall out with me every time I give you advice." Arnold knew that although his dad was trying to support him, he was also receiving a ticking off at the same time.

"Sorry dad, it's been a long week."

"Tell me about it. We have nothing on the scarred man, not a single lead. He has literally vanished into thin air." A tune began playing through the car speakers and the dashboard lit up to say that Mr. Whitaker was calling. His dad answered the call and before he had the chance to speak, Mr. Whitaker had already started talking.

"Arthur, stop whatever you are doing and head to the hospital. Mr. Gray has woken up so I need you to head over and speak with him about his attack."

"Sir, I have Arnold with me. I will head over after I have dropped him off."

"Take the boy with you, he can wait in reception. You won't be there long, and I need you there now." Arthur rolled his eyes which made Arnold laugh.

"Yes sir," he replied.

"Call me as soon as you have seen him." With that, the phone went dead.

Arthur diverted from the route they were taking and began to drive in the direction of the hospital. After around fifteen minutes, they arrived at the infirmary and his dad pulled up in the car park.

"Ridiculous that I have to pay for the parking when I'm working." He grumbled. "Do you want to wait in the car or in the reception area?" Arnold glanced at the temperature gauge in the car and upon realising it was only four degrees outside, he opted to wait in the reception area.

The two of them left the car and made their way to the entrance of the hospital. As they walked through the large automatic double doors, Arnold was faced with the mixed smells of antiseptic and cleaning products, giving the air the distinct fragrance that he associated with hospitals. He looked to his right and noticed row after row of metal chairs that were interconnected, the chairs sporadically filled with people waiting to be seen by the triage nurse. Arnold saw a row that was empty apart from a middle-aged man who was holding his injured arm. Walking over, he sat in the middle of three empty seats not wanting to sit next to anyone that he didn't know.

"Here's some money for a drink and the vending machine is over there. Get yourself something if you want to." Arthur reached into his pocket and pulled out a handful of change, placing it in Arnold's hand. "I shouldn't be too long, maybe around half an hour?" Arthur turned around and headed off down the hospital corridor in the general direction of the ward where Mr. Gray was recovering.

Arnold sat in the waiting area, examining each person sat around him and trying to figure out the different reasons why people were there. There was the man on his row that looked like he may have a broken arm and a toddler a row back with a lump the size of an egg on their head where they must have bumped themselves. The whole while, the antiseptic fragrance continued to engulf his nose and he couldn't decide whether he liked it or hated it.

Another ten minutes went by and Arnold decided that he wanted a drink and a packet of crisps from the vending machine. He couldn't make his mind up if he just wanted to get something out of boredom or need. He stood up and rummaged through his pocket for the change that his dad had given him and sorted through it to find two pound coins; one to get a drink and one to get some crisps from the brightly lit machine. Arnold bought his can of pop and after the noise of it dropping startled an elderly couple sitting nearby, he opened it to take a sip.

He then moved to the next vending machine and looked at the options before tapping A7 into the panel and watching the circular coil behind the crisps start to rotate until the crisps dropped from the shelf. Arnold pushed forward the large letterbox below to grab his snack. Making his way back towards his seat, he thought he saw a familiar face come into the reception area. Arnold watched as the man walked over to the receptionist, before heading off down the same corridor that his dad had taken. The man paused at the bottom of the corridor and appeared to stop a nurse, possibly to ask for directions. Arnold focused and stared down the corridor to try and make out the man's features. After focusing for a couple of seconds, he realised to his surprise that it was his grandad. What was he doing here?

Arnold felt relieved to see him as it had been over a week since the argument with his dad and he had so much to tell him. The relief was followed by confusion; why was his grandad here at the hospital? Taking a big gulp of his can, he then threw it in the bin before shoving the crisp packet he had just bought into his pocket. He set off walking down the corridor, intent on catching up with him. His grandad turned right, then left and then at the bottom of the corridor, he saw his grandad turn left again. Arnold didn't have a clue where he was going and realised that if he lost sight of him, he would most likely need to ask for directions just to get back to the main reception area.

He continued to follow his grandad, choosing not to shout out to him as he didn't want the embarrassment of everyone stopping to look at him; that certainly wouldn't help with his fear of blushing. He walked across the end of the next corridor only to see his grandad walk onto a ward. Who was he here to see? Intrigued, Arnold continued to follow him, however, the auto-lock on the doors had just kicked in as he reached them, stopping him from going any further. Arnold stood there for a moment, wondering what to do next when he saw a cleaner pushing a trolley coming towards him on the other side of the double doors. She pressed a button on the other side and the doors unlocked and opened.

"Can I help you?" she asked, as Arnold began to walk past her.

"Sorry, I'm here to see my grandad," he replied, happy in the knowledge that he hadn't really been that dishonest.

"Ok then, go on." She pushed her trolley through the door and allowed Arnold to pass. Surprised at how easy it was to gain entry Arnold continued down the corridor, looking to the side he noticed a sign that read ward twenty two AMU.

Arnold couldn't help but think he was finally about to get some answers.

Chapter Thirteen

Arnold walked down another corridor looking across each bay of beds to try and find where his grandad had gone. He was walking by a closed-off room when he heard his grandad's muffled voice. Arnold stopped and then moved closer to try and hear what was being said.

"How are you, Charles?" His grandad spoke with concern. "You had me worried, enough to meet with the others. They send their best."

"I'm not going to lie, Alfred, I have felt better," a weary voice replied. "How are you? It has been far too long." Arnold moved to look through the glass panel in the window and saw his grandad and his dad stood on either side of a bed. He could see Charles sat up with a dinner table in front of him. The atmosphere in the room appeared to change as the old man began to speak about his attack. "That man, he knew who I was, and he knew that I used to be a Doyen, I am sure of it!" his voice becoming slightly agitated. "He had the dagger, Alfred. He had the Blade of the Spirits."

His grandad stepped back from Charles in surprise. "Are you absolutely certain? You're saying someone used it to attack you? That can't be - it's impossible. That blade has gone."

"I know exactly when that blade went missing, Alfred. I was there with you." Charles swallowed hard. "I think he knows what we did." Arnold's grandad shook his head.

"That's impossible. No one else knows. There were four of us there that day and your Betsy is no longer with us."

"Don't you mean five?" Charles corrected.

"Arnold spoke of the Blade. He said he had seen a picture in a book that he had found in the Athenaeum and was adamant that the scarred man had it. My god, he was right," Arthur said, clearly shaken. Arnold felt a sense of satisfaction from knowing that he had been right about the Blade, however after witnessing the conversation between the three Doyens, past and present, he had even more questions than before. He now knew there was a link between his grandad, Charles, the scarred man and the Blade of the Spirits but he had no idea why the scarred man would have attacked Charles. His grandad had said they had spent a long time looking for the Blade, so the two of them must have worked together as Doyens years ago. Arnold began to feel concerned about his grandad; if the scarred man had attacked Charles with the Blade that he and his grandad had been looking for, surely there was a possibility that he would also come after his grandad?

Suddenly, there was a loud bang at the auto-lock doors that Arnold had walked through to enter the ward. This was quickly followed by another loud bang and another and then Arnold heard the auto-lock doors swing open, stopping only for the walls on either side as the doors crashed into them. There was silence for a few seconds followed by a scream from a woman further down the corridor and towards the airlock. This was followed by a deafening roar that shook Arnold to the bone. He looked down the corridor to see a large mane-less lion running at speed down the corridor towards him, its giant muscular frame covered with scars, suggesting many battles it had fought and most probably won. Arnold tried to move out of the way, but the large spirit beast crashed into him sending him flying across the corridor and into the nurse's station in the middle of the ward. He winced as he hit the edge of the desk and landed back on the floor.

Dazed, he looked up to see the lion run straight past him. Arnold could hear the muffled screams of the other patients and the staff members on the ward and as he gathered himself, all he could see were legs running past him as everyone ran away from the sound of the growling lion. Its supernatural glow lit up the ward, but nobody was stopping to admire it. Arnold pulled himself to his knees using the nurse station that he had fallen against and looked over at the door where he knew Charles, his grandad and dad were. Beyond the door, he could see a crowd of people scrambling to get away from the lion and then Arnold noticed him. Walking through the crowd slowly, uninterested in the people running past him; it was the scarred man. Arnold could see him walking down the corridor, his gaze moving from one bay to the next as he scanned the area for Charles. He continued to walk through the crowd which had now been reduced to one or two people. He looked over at Arnold, taking in that he was not steady on his feet and was leaning against the nurse's station.

"You," he growled. "What are the chances of that?" The aggression in his voice was thick as he continued to talk. "Luckily, I am not here for you." He stopped at Charles' hospital room.

Suddenly, the door was kicked open and Arthur threw himself at the scarred man, knocking him into the wall.

"Go!" Arthur shouted, as his grandad exited the room with Charles draped over his shoulder. Arnold was momentarily impressed with the ease with which he appeared to be carrying Charles. His grandad began to make his way towards the broken auto-lock doors at the entrance to the ward. Arnold then panicked as he realised that his dad had not seen him and had no idea he was on the ward. He tried to call out but was still winded from the lion running into him meaning no sound came from his mouth.

"You won't stop me," the scarred man growled, staring into Arthur's dark eyes who in turn, returned a ferocious gaze. He pushed back against Arthur, before freeing an arm and striking him across the face. He attempted to strike again but Arthur blocked it and aimed a blow into the midriff of the scarred man who let out a loud gasp as his fist made contact. The scarred man looked infuriated and his eyes began to bulge, pushing Arthur back with considerable force and knocking him backwards into the wall behind him. The scarred man then let loose with a flurry of blows to his body, with Arthur managing to block the odd one before he took a blow to the head. Arthur fell to the floor and the scarred man grabbed him by his clothes before throwing him at the opposite wall. Arnold's dad lay motionless, rendered unconscious from the attack. The scarred man turned and began to walk in the direction of Charles and his grandad.

"Come!" he commanded loudly, Arnold instantly realising who, or what, he was talking to.

Arnold heard the heavy sound of giant paws as the lion made its way back down the corridor. Knowing he needed to do something to help his grandad, Arnold looked around at the ward, hoping for inspiration. He hopped over the desk at the nurse's station and began to push it out into the corridor, but the weight of it was making it difficult. Realising he didn't have long, he turned and moved his back against it, bracing his legs and pushing against the desk with as much strength as he could muster. Arnold's muscles were burning as he attempted to move the station, but he could feel it starting to move. He felt the force as the lion crashed into it, the desk knocking the spirit beast further down the corridor and leaving Arnold sprawled out on the floor. He could hear the breathing of the lion that was now lying just feet from where he lay.

Climbing to his feet as fast as he could, he looked around to find the scarred man, but he was already out of sight. To his horror, the exit route was now blocked by the upturned nurse's station which left him stranded in the ward with the giant lion spirit beast. Panicked, he jumped backwards to create some distance between him and the lion which was still lying on the floor but was beginning to gather itself.

His chest felt tight as he tried to steady his breathing, placing his hand over his mouth to quieten himself. Spotting some more doors with a fire escape light above it, he glanced over at the lion and saw it was getting to his feet. Arnold slowly began to walk towards the fire escape, trying his hardest to do this as silently as he could. He hoped his dad was ok as the lion couldn't get past the upturned desk without forcing it. He continued to creep towards the fire exit in front of him.

Hearing a low grumbling noise, Arnold looked to his right, disorientated as the lion was to his left. His adrenaline spiked and he could hear his heartbeat as blood pumped around his body at an elevated rate. Stood by a large window at the top of the ward was a second lion of the same size and without a mane. His heart sank as he realised that the lion had his eyes firmly fixed on him and nothing else. Arnold could see there was no one else left on this ward apart from him; he was the prey. So, he thought. *'How do you outrun a lion?'*

The lion let out a blood-curdling roar that almost knocked Arnold's legs from underneath him and his whole body began trembling with fear. Setting off at pace he made for the fire escape with the lion following. Slamming his hands against the metal bar that ran through the middle of the door, Arnold forced it open, nearly taking the bar clean off the door. The door burst open and he began to run as fast as he could down the concrete steps, two at a time. He reached the bottom of the first row of steps and looked up at the door as the lion ran through it, leaping through the air at Arnold, clearing all the steps with ease.

'Run!'

Arnold began running down the next row of steps as the lion smashed into the wall behind him. He reached the bottom as the lion cleared the next row of steps, this time Arnold just managing to roll out of the way as the lion thumped against the wall. Climbing to his feet, Arnold stared over the side of the railings and knew he could not outrun the lion. He needed to think fast but he needed to move even faster. Seeing no other option, he grabbed hold of the rail as his brain sent him messages - 'What are you doing?', 'This is mad!' and 'You can do this!'

He gathered himself and took a deep breath before climbing over the rail and dropping to the floor below. The sensation of weightlessness came over him for a brief moment, before crumpling into the floor with a sickening thud. He let out a gasp as the air inside him exited instantly and he realised he had winded himself again. He pulled himself up using the railing and a sharp pain told him he had injured his ankle and was now struggling to walk, never mind run, the throbbing pain travelling far up his leg.

Hearing the lion jump down the next row of stairs, Arnold knew he had no option but to do the same again. He rolled over the top of the railings again just as the lion drew level with him, slamming into the floor and landing on his side. The wind was well and truly knocked out of him now and he instantly knew that he had done something to his arm this time. The searing pain was spreading from his shoulder downwards, but he knew he needed to get up to his feet quickly, otherwise, the lion would be upon him. Dazed, dizzy and in an immense amount of pain he didn't feel that he had anything left in him; his energy was drained, his body broken. His brain had other ideas, however. *'Get up Arnold! Get up and get through those doors!'*

He had made it to here and fought against every muscle in his body to stand up but he somehow managed to muster enough strength to climb to his feet once more. He realised he was now on the ground floor, given that there were no more steps leading downwards, and he could see the emergency exit just a few feet away.

'Move!'

Limping heavily, he made his way towards the exit, the taste of blood in his mouth. He could feel himself beginning to lose his balance as his legs began to give way, feeling as if they were glued to the floor. Exhausted, he threw himself as hard as he could against the exit, forcing it open and falling through it onto the solid ground outside. Arnold rolled onto his back, in agony and with no energy left. He had never felt anything like the fear and pain that he was currently experiencing. His heart continued to race as he thought about what to do next; he had managed to escape so far but now he was fresh out of ideas. Lying in the darkness, Arnold could hear the soft rumble of the lion as it slowly made its way outside. It was calm, collected and it was stalking him. It was hunting him. Its eyes fixed on Arnold as it crouched and began to crawl towards him ready to strike. Arnold closed his eyes, bracing himself for a blow that surely would mean the end of him.

A loud roar filled the air which shook Arnold to his bones, but this roar sounded different to the lions and Arnold did not recognise it. He opened his eyes to see a large bear spirit beast smash into the side of the spectral lion knocking it off its feet. The bear continued its charge and ran at the lion standing on its back legs to strike it with considerable force. The lion growled as the grizzly bear bored into its side. The lion quickly got back up and the bear quickly jumped back to its feet. The lion stood and let out a thunderous roar which the grizzly bear greeted with its own equally deafening battle cry, the two of them bearing their razor-sharp teeth at each other.

Leaping through the air with its intensely muscular legs, the lion landed on the bear and instantly sank its knife-like teeth into its back, the bear let out a groaning noise as it attempted to shake it off. The light-emitting from the two spirit beasts was fully illuminating the area where they fought, Arnold unable to see outside the periphery due to the darkness of the night sky.

He had never seen the grizzly bear spirit beast but was sure that it was his dad's, the awe-inspiring beast was more than holding its own against the giant lion. The bear and the lion continued to grapple with each other, both trading blows with one another with their huge, shovel-like paws. Claws drawn, they continued to swipe at each other's heads, with the bear looking as if it was beginning to get the upper hand. This was until the second lion exited the building, making its way to join the battle. It began to run at speed, ready to protect its brother.

"The second one's here!" Arnold screamed, trying to alert the bear spirit beast but it was too late. Within a moment, the second lion had run into the fracas and lunged at the bear, clawing it all the way down its back. The bear let out an ear-piercing roar of pain and the two lions began to pummel it, their claws piercing the spectral animal's thick natural armour as if shredding paper.

The bear tried in vain to fight back against the two lions, but it visibly began to slow, its wounds from the battle taking its toll. One of the lions jumped towards it and the bear managed to bite the lion and used its own momentum to throw it past him. However, as it did this, the other lion was quickly upon the bear, slamming its body into the bear's head and knocking it to the floor. Sensing the bear's fading power, the two lions crouched down, staring at it and waiting to pounce.

Arnold watched the fight feeling tense, injured and unable to do anything to help. He felt completely powerless. The lions were now teasing the bear, dragging out their final attack and causing Arnold to feel even more useless. The final blow didn't come, however, as suddenly the two lions stopped and ran off into the field next to the hospital, the light glow around them becoming smaller and smaller as they vanished into the distance.

Arnold could hear a low grumble emitting from the grizzly bear that had just saved his life and he was relieved as he saw it push itself to its feet. The bear looked over to Arnold and began to walk towards him slowly and Arnold felt as though the pain he was feeling was becoming less and less. The closer the bear got, the more his fear and anxiety lifted. The bear was calming him, reassuring him but without saying any words. It was a strange sensation, but it felt as though he was healing. Attempting to stand up, he quickly realised his ankle wasn't giving way and he didn't fall back to the floor. The bear continued to walk over, lowering its head. Arnold reached out to touch it and instantly felt the throbbing in his ankle stop. The bear grumbled at Arnold and pushed its giant head against him, further comforting him. The sensation was indescribable; a mixture of reality and spectre, a mixed feeling of something being there but not at the same time. The bear sat down wrapping its great arms around Arnold, continuing to soothe his pain. It was waiting for help to come and was going to stay with Arnold until it arrived. He felt a strange feeling of warmth continue to cover him with rhythmic vibrating waves pulsating through him; he felt as though he could just go to sleep, he was that comfortable. He was closing his eyes when he began to hear the calls in the distance.

"Arnold, Arnold, can you hear me?" Arthur was shouting as loud as he could, the panic in his voice obvious.

"Over there, Arthur! I can see your spirit beast." Arnold recognised the second voice as that of his grandad. The thought of them both being there brought further warmth to Arnold and the reassurance he was safe at last. His dad reached him first, dropping to his knees and taking hold of him.

"Are you ok? Where are you injured?" he asked, anxiously checking

Arnold for wounds. "I saw you run through the exit with the lions, I thought you were-" Arthur scooped his arms around him and embraced his son. Arnold hadn't received a hug like this for a long time and he needed it. He began to cry, the experience and his emotions catching up with him. "Thank you," His dad said gently, as he reached out his hand and placed it on his spirit beast's head. With this, the grizzly bear began to slowly disappear, absorbing back into Arthur's body.

A few moments passed and his grandad had caught up to the two of them, lowering his hands to his knees he stopped to catch his breath.

"He's gone. He escaped, vanished," His grandad panted. "But he got what he came for. Charles is dead."

Chapter Fourteen

Arnold spent the next six weeks recovering from his meeting with the scarred man and the Lions of Tsavo. Between school and spending his evenings in the Athenaeum, there was not much else that Arnold was able to do, as his arm was out of commission, other than read. He had received a hairline fracture in his arm and badly sprained his ankle in the encounter but had been very well taken care of between the efforts of his mum and Everett. She had been coming around at the weekends to help Arnold complete his homework, given that he couldn't write. Arnold had hated having his arm in a cast over the recent weeks not just because of the limitations this put on him, but also for the insanity-inducing itch he would often experience halfway down his arm. He had, however, enjoyed the company he had been receiving from Everett. The two of them were getting along better than ever and Arnold was fast coming to the realisation that they seemed to have a lot in common.

Evenings at the Athenaeum had been slow, with Arnold spending his time trying to find out more on the Lions of Tsavo and the Blade of the Spirits. Unfortunately, he only had the one book that he had found by Betsy Devon to research. He had now read the book from front to back, twice over. In the latter pages of the chapter around the Blade of the Spirits, the book had confirmed the story that his dad had told both boys on the night of the attack. The rest of the book just listed different expeditions in which Betsy and the team she was with had been on, attempting to uncover varying artefacts from around the world. In truth, Arnold had not shown much interest in the other expeditions, only really wanting to know more about the Blade of the Spirits.

Arnold's readings and research had got him no closer in finding out more about the Blade, the Lions or the scarred man and what linked them to Charles. Arnold had not attended Charles' funeral, as he didn't know Charles except for the chance encounter on his birthday. His dad and grandad had attended with his grandad suffering the most anguish from his old colleague's death. Arnold had seen his grandad quite often over the last few weeks, as he would call around for a cup of tea and check in on Arnold's recovery. Arnold hadn't had time alone with his grandad to talk to him about Charles and how the two of them knew each other and whenever he tried to broach the topic with him, his grandad would change the subject. Now he was feeling back to normal, Arnold had planned to call round one evening after school to catch up with him and try again at getting more information out of him. However, it was like trying to crack the hardest of safes. His grandad's stubbornness was certainly a trait Arnold shared and he was not going to give up until he found out everything he wanted to know.

More frustrating than anything, Arnold had not had any more dreams about flying since the attack. He craved the thrill of flying so badly and would do anything to experience it again. Despite all this, Arnold had been looking forward to today, specifically 11.20am. He had been crossing off the days on his calendar in anticipation; today was the day he had his cast taken off. He had spent the morning at school and his dad was due to pick him up at around half-past ten to take him up to the hospital for his appointment. Standing outside the school gates, his bag draped over his left shoulder as his right arm was in a sling, a gust of wind caught the inside of his blazer giving him a sharp reminder of the chill he would experience when flying.

After around five minutes, Arnold saw the blue ford focus come around the corner, recognising it instantly as his dad's car. Arthur pulled up and opened the door so Arnold could climb in, placing his bag in the passenger side footwell by his feet.

"All set?" Arthur asked. He was dressed in a smart blue suit with a pinstriped shirt having just left work to take him to his appointment.

"I can't wait," he replied, looking forward more to giving his arm a good itch than anything else. It had been seriously driving him mad.

They made it to the hospital in good time and after signing in with the receptionist in the fracture clinic, they sat waiting on a small row of seats. Not too long later, he found himself sat in the consultant's room with the doctor using the large sheers to cut off the plaster cast. The relief Arnold felt once it was removed was fantastic and he instantly started itching a spot on the inside of his arm that had been driving him mad for the last six weeks.

"Now, your cast is off, but you still need to rest it for a couple of weeks." The doctor spoke in a patronising manner, as though Arnold was about to start doing handstands and cartwheels as soon as he left the room. "Try not to do anything too strenuous. It might ache a bit now the cast is off, but it is nothing that some paracetamol will not fix." The doctor then asked Arnold to move his arm around in multiple positions and rotations before deciding he was happy with his movement and discharged him. Arnold left the hospital with his dad and made the short walk back to the car, rotating his shoulder and trying to get used to having free movement without the cast weighing it down. His arm felt so much lighter now which was a bit of a strange sensation. Climbing into the car, Arnold sighed at the prospect of having to go back to school. He picked his bag up from the footwell and took out his planner to see what his afternoon sessions were; Geography and Cooking. Yuk.

Arthur started the car and set off, ready to drop Arnold back at school and head back to work.

"It was a bit traumatic that," Arthur said while reversing out of the parking bay. Arnold looked at the side of his dad's face, wondering if he had actually been with him. The removing of the cast had been the most un-traumatic thing to happen to him lately compared to his birthday, the Ch'ahb' and throwing himself down two flights of stairs while trying to outrun the Lions of Tsavo. Arthur smiled which slowly turned into a grin "Think you need to take the rest of the day off, son. Let's call it a wellbeing day." He finished reversing the car and winked at Arnold and the two smiled at each other.

Only one thought crossed his mind now he had some free time.

'I could go and see grandad.'

The journey home was quick and soon Arnold was jumping out of the car and waving his dad off back to work. Arnold went inside, dumped his backpack just past the front door and ran upstairs to his bedroom. After throwing on some jeans and his Everton FC football shirt, he ran back downstairs to make himself a quick sandwich, before heading out the front door to make his way to his grandad's house. He thought he might ring to let him know he was on his way over but then decided against it as his grandad very rarely answered his phone anyway.

It was a lovely day and the sun was casting large shadows from the buildings and trees all around Arnold as he walked to his grandad's. The heat was very welcome as it had not been the warmest of years so far and it was a nice feeling as the sun-warmed Arnold's face and arms. It brought back memories of the strange sensation he had experienced when his dad's spirit beast had held him to soothe him when he lay on the floor injured.

He made his way to his grandad's house which sat at the bottom of a pristinely kept cul de sac.

Walking up to the front of the semi-detached house that he lived in, Arnold knocked on the brown, wooden door and stood waiting for his grandad to answer. He could feel the heat of the sun on the back of his head; it still felt soothing to feel it against his skin. There was no answer, so Arnold knocked again, this time slightly harder just in case his grandad hadn't heard him. When there was no answer again, Arnold decided to try the front door, thinking that if it was locked, he may have gone out for something. Pushing the door handle downwards, he then pushed against the door to see if it would open and it did, the door creaking slowly open before he stepped inside. Moving into the hallway, he realised that his grandad was sat fast asleep in his armchair, the low grumbling noise coming from his nose showing he was in a deep sleep.

Glancing upstairs as he passed the stairs, he noticed something different that caught his eye. The loft hatch was open, with a set of steps leading up to them. This was puzzling, given that he had never known his grandad to ever use his loft space. Intrigued as to what his grandad had been doing up there, he had an overwhelming urge to have a look. 'It won't cause any harm to have a look' he reasoned, sneaking up the stairs whilst trying his hardest not to disturb his grandad. The stairs creaking ever so slightly as he made his way towards the top. Halfway up, Arnold's grandad stirred causing him to freeze in his tracks, trying desperately not to wake him. After a few moments of shuffling around his grandad began snoring again and Arnold set off to the top of the stairs once more, each step creaking slowly as he put his foot on them. Arnold stood at the bottom of the loft ladder, more curious than ever at what might be in the loft. All he had to do now was climb the rungs without disturbing his grandad. He took a deep breath and pulled himself onto the ladder, surprised how sturdy they were which made it easier than expected to reach the top. Grabbing hold of the wooden ledge he pulled himself up through the loft space, pushing up from his knees to a standing position.

The room was dark, and Arnold was unable to see anything. There was a damp musty smell in the air that left a bitter taste as he drew a breath. Taking a step forward slowly he held his hands out in front of him and felt what he presumed was a pull-cord light switch. He took hold of it and tugged on it lightly just to make sure it was in fact connected to the ceiling above him. It was, so Arnold pulled the cord until it clicked, indicating the light had been activated. He waited for a second and the light above him began to flicker before switching on and illuminating the room.

"Wow." Arnold sighed, he had not known what to expect, most likely boxes and bags of rubbish. He was taken aback by what he could see in the room. It had clearly not been in frequent use given the thick layer of dust that sat on top of everything, but it looked as though the contents of the attic belonged in a museum. There were glass cases on either side of the room, with varying objects in them from vases to pieces of armour. Arnold wasn't sure where any of this stuff came from, but he was very sure that it was seriously cool. Arnold surveyed the room while taking in all the different objects and his eyes were drawn to footprints that led to the corner of the room. Guessing this was where his grandad must have been most recently, Arnold followed the tracks.

In the corner of the room sat an old wooden trunk, the rusted metal frame around the edges barely visible through the dirt that had collated on top of it over the years. There was a padlock on the trunk but on closer inspection, the key was still inside. Intrigued, Arnold turned the key until the padlock clicked open. Removing the padlock, the hinges creaked as he opened the chest slowly, still not wanting to disturb his grandad. Once opened, Arnold was unable to see clearly due to the position of the trunk and his own shadow, making it hard to make out what sat within the darkness. He repositioned himself to allow some light past and Arnold noticed what looked like an old photograph. Arnold picked it up to examine it closer. The photo was not complete, with a section of it torn off, but he could clearly make out his much younger looking grandad with two other people from what Arnold presumed was a holiday somewhere. Arnold knew his grandad liked visiting countries all over the world and judging by his clothing and the giant tree he was stood in front of, he thought this was from somewhere in a forest. Arnold placed the torn photo to his side and saw that there was a long item wrapped in a red cloth. Arnold reached in, eager to see what it was and found that it was quite heavy. Leaning into the trunk with both hands he removed the weighty object, before turning and placing it on the dust-laden floor. Curious, he began to unfold the cloth which surrounded it, feeling a strange pull to the item that he couldn't quite put his finger on. After removing the cloth, he stared at the item not knowing what exactly it was. To Arnold, it looked like a weapon, and an old one at that. It resembled a cricket bat, though both sides were flat and etched with intricate carvings that Arnold had recently seen at the Chichen. They were hieroglyphs. Each side appeared to be animal totems etched into the dark stained wood, however, Arnold was unable to make out what they were. The hilt was bound with a maroon material and at the bottom of the hilt, there were more intricate carvings. Around the outer edge of the paddle-like object was finely polished black stone, which had been inserted into the wood all the way around. The end result meant it looked not too dissimilar from the blades wrapped around a chainsaw. This was the strangest looking thing that he had ever seen, and he was bemused by what it was and what it was doing in his grandad's attic.

Pick it up.

The pull to the artefact felt stronger than ever and he grabbed hold of the hilt, ready to pick it up. As he grasped the hilt, a surge of energy ran through his arm which startled him into letting go of it and dropping it to the floor with a dull thud. Arnold stopped for a moment, thinking that something felt strange and different than before. It only took a moment for him to realise that the background noise from his grandad snoring had stopped. Arnold spun around to find his grandad's head poking through the loft hatch, frowning at him. Arnold had been that engrossed in the object he had discovered that he had not heard his grandad coming up the stairs or the ladder.

"Thought you were a bloody burglar," his grandad huffed. "Why on earth are you not at school and more to the point, why are you up here?"

"I had my cast taken off and dad said I didn't have to go back to school so I thought I would call here. You were asleep and the loft was open, so I wanted to have a look." Arnold's gaze was drawn back to the object on the floor. His grandad saw what he was looking at and let out a sigh. "I suppose you want to know what it is? It's called a Macuahuitl".

"A Mac-a-" Arnold couldn't repeat what his grandad had just said.

"Mac-ua-hu-itl," he repeated. "It's a very old weapon. I stumbled across it years ago when I was a young Doyen. "I kept it, even used it a couple of times in combat. It's stronger than it looks, you know. I took it everywhere with me once I found it." Arnold was aghast at what his grandad had just said.

"In combat?" His grandad never spoke much about when he was a Doyen.

"Yes, combat. It happens sometimes when you are a Doyen. Back then anyway. Not so much now as back in my time, thank goodness." Arnold didn't know what to say. He couldn't imagine his grandad in combat let alone swinging this macuahuitl thing around. His grandad had never really discussed his Doyen days with him, and he felt as though he didn't want to miss this opportunity. He listened quietly, waiting for his grandad to continue. "That sword has got me out of some serious trouble."

"It's the most bizarre weapon I have ever seen," said Arnold, the unique shape of the weapon really catching Arnold's attention. "What is it made out of?" He asked, wanting to know more about the relic as he continued to feel drawn to it and unable to take his eyes off it.

"Well the wood, as you can see, has no blemishes on it despite being used. This is because of the ancient way the wood was treated. Or at least that's my theory. I never found any solid evidence of it." He chuckled like he had an in-joke with himself that only a few people would understand. "The sharpened stone that's inserted around the outer edge of the sword is called obsidian. It is highly polished and, again, if treated the right way it enables this sword to be just as lethal as any sword cast from iron or steel. When used properly, anyway." Arnold didn't know what to think. His grandad rarely spoke about his past days as a Doyen, but now Arnold had found this ancient cache of relics and weapons in his loft, he suddenly seemed animated and keen to discuss it.

"Why is all this stuff up here, grandad?" Arnold stepped towards a glass case that had an old vase sat inside it. It looked basic with no etchings or intricate carvings on it but it looked old. Really old. "I thought the Chichen would want all of these?" He rubbed his hand on the glass to brush some of the dust that had gathered on the front of the glass casing. His grandad sighed.

"As I progressed in the Chichen, I came to realise that they didn't need to know about everything." His grandad walked over to the middle of the loft space and wrapped the Macuahuitl back up in the cloth that it lay on before picking it up and walking over to the chest to place it back inside. "I used to enjoy collecting things. There used to be a purpose but, in the end, well... it just ended up in here." He turned to face Arnold. "There is stuff up here that the Chichen has no idea about. Relics and artefacts from all over the world, your grandma and I-" He stopped himself from talking further. He never spoke about his Doyen days and he never so much as acknowledged his wife. Arnold had no idea what she looked like as his grandad had no photos of her on display. His dad had always told him that the memories of her were simply too painful for them both when she had passed. Arnold had little information on her but everything he knew had come from his dad, who himself seemed to know very little of his own mum. He had learned not to ask questions growing up, knowing how much it hurt his grandad to talk about her, so his grandma had faded away into history as though she had never existed. Arnold had always respected this for his grandad's sake, but Arnold had always had a burning desire to find out more about her. Sensing the opportunity, he seized the moment to ask something he had never dared to ask before.

"What happened to her, grandad?" There was a softness to Arnold's voice, not wanting to upset his grandad but also desperate to know more about his grandma.

"Forty years." His grandad let out a sigh as though defeated as if the two words he had just spoken had taken a tremendous weight off his shoulders. "It has been forty years since I last saw her." He closed the trunk where he had just placed the Macuahuitl and sat on top of the lid. He exhaled. Arnold could not believe it. His grandad was opening up to him about his grandma. Eager to listen, Arnold grabbed a footstool that he could see at the far end of the loft and moved it further into the centre of the room, before wiping off the dust. It left a small plume of dirt floating around in the air and he could taste it slightly as he sat and took in a deep breath in anticipation of what his grandad was about to tell him. "We were in Africa at the time, a few of us. It was part holiday and part exploration; that's what we liked to do back then. Well, what we needed to do. Your dad was actually with us and it was the first time that we had taken him away. In fact, it was the first time we had been away since the day he was born." A smile passed over his face at the thought of the happiness they had once experienced at becoming parents for the first time. "Your grandma and I had always wanted to visit Africa and we had decided that we would join a few of our friends that had invited us over to see them. They had been working over there for about a year".

"Charles?"

"Yes, Charles and his wife." His grandad's voice had become stronger and the words came out of his mouth more smoothly, not forced. "Arthur was two years old and a right handful. Just like you used to be." His grandad chuckled again. "He could walk and was beginning to start forming words for the first time...everything he saw he wanted, and you needed to keep an eye on him because he was as quick as a flash." Arnold sat on the footstool, eyes completely fixed on his grandad. He was totally engrossed in the story that he was being told.

"Charles' wife wanted to go visit an old temple, so we decided to tag along for the experience hoping to learn more about the local culture. That's when everything went wrong." His grandad began to look pained and his voice began to tremble. "You see, your grandma was the most beautiful woman I had ever seen and the only thing that matched her beauty was the fierceness with which she would protect her family." His grandad was struggling to talk about her now and for a moment Arnold considered stopping him, seeing the pain he was going through from the conversation they were having. He exhaled. "She was a dragon, Arnold. Well at least her spirit beast was." Arnold nearly fell from the footstool he was perched on. Dragon spirit beasts were somewhat of an unknown quantity, having been so few known throughout history. One thing that was known was the fiery rage that history would say the bearers of this spirit beast possessed. Arnold gathered himself and continued to listen to what his grandad had to say. "She was an amazing person Arnold. She was kind and loving and caring and just wanted to do right by everyone." His voice was sharp and direct as if he was defending her. "As you know, the dragon spirit beast is the rarest form of a spirit beast. No one has ever known anyone to have one, not in recent generations anyway. That is, apart from me and your grandma. Your grandma had kept this hidden from everyone, even her own family." Arnold swallowed. He could feel a lump in his throat as his emotions were high. He was learning about a woman that, if not for her, he wouldn't exist.

"Why?" he asked, not understanding fully what his grandad was alluding to. "Why would she not tell anyone?"

"Because she would have been taken away, experimented on like some lab rat by the Chichen. They would want to know the source of her power." There was anger in his voice now. "Dragon spirit beasts are feared. Some people may have even tried to kill her because of it, because of the power it gave her. So, your grandma kept it hidden inside her, never used it, never needed to until the day that we lost her. We were in Africa and to everyone over here we were on holiday but really, we were looking for an artefact. Like we did every summer but this one was special though. Our research led us to believe that the blade we were looking for could trap her spirit beast inside. She would have become a menial, but she would have been safe and it is what your grandma wanted. All I can say is that we found the blade, we had it in our hands and that is when her spirit beast took over. It did not wish to be trapped and so it corrupted her."

"Corrupted?"

"Yes, it took control of her mind and her body. Just like that she was gone, forever in her place was this vile spirit beast that only knew anger and fury. It attacked us as it was desperate to escape, and we had no option but to defend ourselves."

Arnold stood up, he was upset about his grandma, part of him confused as to why he was suddenly being told all this. "Why now? Why are you suddenly talking to me about her?" Arnold could feel the warmth of the tears that were rolling down his cheeks. He felt completely overwhelmed by the situation. He continued to focus on his grandad who also had tears running down his face.

"Because I'm scared, Arnold. I'm absolutely petrified," he responded, looking completely vulnerable.

"What of?"

"You." Arnold sat back down, confused by his grandad's words. Why would he be scared of him? Arnold would never hurt his grandad in a million years; he was the most important person in the world to him. His grandad wiped away the tears from his cheek and sniffed what must have been a runny nose, his face becoming blotchy from his released emotions. "Your dreams, Arnold. It's your dreams." He gathered himself before continuing, "Your grandma used to tell me about these vivid dreams of flying that she used to have when she was younger, even speaking of a tower that kept recurring in her dream. Your dad told me all about your Ch'ahb' and your split auro...you showed the sign of the dragon and you're having the same dreams that your grandma had."

Arnold suddenly realised what his grandad was suggesting. So much had happened recently that he had not been looking into the identity of his spirit beast. He had solely been focusing on the Blade of the Spirit World, the scarred man and the Lions of Tsavo.

"You think I have a dragon spirit beast, don't you?" His grandad nodded.

"Yes, Arnold and it absolutely fills me with dread." His grandad wasn't holding back with his words now, causing more confusion for Arnold.

"Why? What is so bad about it? It might be rare, but I am sure I could handle it." A slight cockiness was coming over him with the realisation he may have the rarest of spirit beasts inside of him. His grandad stood up and brushed off the dust that had settled on top of his legs. He walked across to the glass cabinet where the bowl Arnold had looked at earlier was placed. Arnold spun on the footstool to face the back of his grandad, only seeing part of his face in the form of a reflection in the glass panel Arnold had earlier wiped the dust from.

"Your grandma was the nicest, kindest person that I have ever come across. She was simple, beautiful - inside and out. That, that thing still consumed her to protect itself. She had no control over it." His voice became slightly raised, there was no mistake of the anger he felt. "It took her away from us, that dragon spirit beast, and I think that it lies within you too, Arnold. That is what scares me more than anything on this earth; the thought of it corrupting you too. You know what happens if you are corrupted? You lose all control, the spirit beast takes over as if you were a puppet, unable to ever escape. The Chichen knows that you may have a dragon spirit beast and that means they are watching you, closer than you could imagine. I won't let them take you away."

Arnold didn't know what to say to his grandad. He felt there was more to what his grandad was telling him but didn't feel that he could take any more information in. He truly felt at saturation point, a sponge that was holding as much water as possible and he did not want to start leaking out what he had just been told. Arnold stood up and walked over to his grandad and gave him the tightest hug he could muster. His grandad placed his arms around Arnold and squeezed him back and Arnold felt comforted as if wrapped in a warm blanket. He knew his grandad would protect him from anything, he always had since he was little. He felt safe when he was with him and he wanted his grandad to feel the same around him now that he was older. He wanted him to know that he was going to be ok, that everything was going to be ok. Arnold knew that his grandad's concerns must be severe for him to talk to him about his grandma but for now he had no more questions. For now, in this moment, he simply wanted to comfort his grandad to help him offload the unbearable weight he had been keeping to himself for so many years. The two cried together, taking comfort from one another.

What if I could control it?

Chapter Fifteen

Arnold was back at home and in a state of shock. His grandma had a dragon spirit beast, the rarest most dangerous form a spirit beast could take, and his grandad was worried that Arnold also had this spirit beast inside of him. That was a lot to take in though the conversation had answered some of the burning questions he had from the night he heard his dad and grandad arguing. He now understood why his grandad had been so against him beginning training, too. It was because of the risk associated with having a dragon spirit beast. It had destroyed his grandma and he didn't want it to destroy him, too. His grandad's fears were fair; if he was indeed like his grandma and had a dragon spirit beast, he would have to learn to hide it as she had done, learn to suppress it so that the power of it did not take over. History could not repeat itself.

Arnold lay on his bed staring up at the ceiling, once again his thoughts whirling around in his head. He was beginning to get answers but did not like the way they were going. He had been obsessed with his spirit beast for as long as he could remember, cursing his luck at not developing like his friends were and not becoming in-tune with his auro the same as the others. And now, his spirit beast could be a dragon, something he would have to hide his entire life and on top of that, he would be unable to become a Doyen. He would have to pretend to be a menial, to act as though he had no spirit beast connected to him.

Feeling his frustration building inside, he began to wonder if this was why he had a bit of a temper and experienced fits of jealousy towards his friends like he had been doing recently. At least that would make sense he told himself, trying to justify the whirlwind of emotions he had been experiencing lately. It was all a bit much but at least now he understood his family were trying to shield him from the truth. His dad must have already known about his grandma and had a different way of wanting to protect him and clearly, this was the issue that had caused the argument between him and his grandad a couple of months ago. Weirdly though, his dad must have been prepared for him to learn about it all as he had given his blessing for Arnold to speak with his grandad about it, before the attack at the hospital.

Arnold looked at his watch realising that school had finished and before too long he would need to head to the Chichen and meet up with Otto. His grandad had warned him not to discuss the dragon with anyone, however, Otto was next to him at the Ch'ahb' and witnessed the dragon symbol that had illuminated above Arnold during the ritual. He needed to get ready and meet his friend to offload more than usual; he felt as though his head was going to explode due to the amount of information he was trying to process. At least Otto could try and help him pick things apart or even help him do a bit more research, he told himself as he sat up in his bed.

There was a knock at the front door, soft enough to know that it wasn't Otto and distinct enough to recognise who it was. He had become accustomed to the firm knock that signaled Everett's visits while he had his cast on and a smile came to Arnold's face as his mood lifted. Arnold skipped down the stairs but slowed his pace as he arrived at the front door, trying his hardest to play it cool as he opened it.

And there was Everett, her warm smile instantly lifting him. The sun caught her perfectly soft, dark skin ensuring that her bright blue eyes shone brighter than he had ever seen them.

'What is wrong with you? Stop smiling or you will give her the creeps.'

"Come in." He pulled the door further back and stepped to the side, allowing her to enter the house.

She smiled and stepped through.

"I just wanted to see how the big day had gone. How's it feeling?"

Momentarily Arnold did not have a clue what Everett was talking about as so much had happened today that the fact that he'd had his cast removed felt like a distant memory. He rotated his shoulder and felt his arm ache slightly. He hadn't even noticed the dull pain as his mind had been that busy but suddenly, now he had been reminded of it, it felt like it was catching up with him and it began to throb quite heavily. He felt a wave of nausea washing over him, but Arnold tried to play it cool.

"It's fine. The Doctor said I have to take it easy still for a while, but I will be back to my best soon."

"You won't need me to come around to help with your homework anymore then, will you?" There was a playfulness in Everett's voice that made Arnold realise she was flirting with him, her words almost teasing him and prompting him for another answer. Arnold began to stutter. He so wished for a moment that Otto was here as he would have spoken on his behalf, but he needed to learn to keep calm in these situations, just like he would. He needed to channel his inner Otto.

"You can still come round." He spoke quickly and hurriedly; he couldn't have sounded any less like Otto. "We can do our homework together." He paused for a moment not feeling confident of Everett's response as she didn't reply instantaneously. "That's if you want to."

"Do you want me to?" she replied playfully. Sensing that Everett was fishing for answers from Arnold, his confidence grew.

"Yeah, I do," he smiled, realising that she actually looked just as nervous as he did. "Everett, I just wanted to say thanks for helping me."

"You don't need to thank me."

"But I wanted to. I would be behind on a lot of my work if you hadn't have helped me."

"It would have been cruel to leave Otto to help you do your work." She laughed to herself. "No one deserves that."

"True." They both laughed. Everett grabbed her bag.

"I just wanted to pop by and see how your arm was with the cast off, so I guess I best get going."

"Wait there, just for a moment." Arnold shot up the stairs and returned quickly with a box of chocolates in his hand. "Er, I got these for you, you know, to say thanks."

"Sweet." Everett smiled at Arnold appreciating the gift he had got her. "I'm surprised you came up with that yourself," Arnold smirked. "You didn't, did you?"

"That would be telling." Arnold grinned, knowing full well it was his grandad's idea. Everett stepped forward and placed a gentle kiss on Arnold's cheek, his face immediately beginning to colour. Everett stood back and smiled at Arnold again and suddenly he felt like he had all the confidence in the world, like he could achieve anything he desired.

"See you at school tomorrow," she called as she left and headed off home leaving Arnold stood there with a goofy smile. He was experiencing happiness, something that had been missing from his life for a while now. Finally, something positive. Arnold felt on top of the world as he looked at his watch and realised he needed to get to the Chichen. He grabbed his jacket, put his shoes on and locked the house up before making his way to meet Otto.

Arnold was in a daze. Everett had kissed him on the cheek. A girl had given him a kiss! He could not believe it and Arnold felt on top of the world. On his short walk to the Chichen, Arnold's worries about potentially having a dragon spirit beast drifted momentarily to the back of his mind.

Chapter Sixteen

Arnold arrived at the Chichen and greeted Sue in his usual manner as he made his way to the Athenaeum. She flashed him a smile. Arnold felt like he had a spring in his step, a swagger he had never had before, and he liked this feeling. He placed his finger on the pressure pad and the glass double doors unfrosted before opening. Arnold could see Otto pressing the screen on the table in the centre of the Athenaeum, determined as ever to get into it.

"You're never going to get in," he called out Otto who stopped what he was doing and turned to face him.

"What's happened to you? You look different," Otto asked curiously, realising that Arnold had an unfamiliar confident air about him.

"Everett kissed me." Otto stared.

"Seriously? She kissed you?"

"Yup." Arnold wished he had thought about his reply before speaking but he hadn't and would have to deal with how cringeworthy that sounded out loud. "And my cast is off."

"Sounds like a belting day!" Otto winked at him, the best way he could show his pride in Arnold receiving his first kiss from a girl.

"And that's not the half of it - there's so much more that I need to tell you." Arnold proceeded to tell Otto about his grandad's loft space, the Macuahuitl, his grandma and her dragon spirit beast.

"That's a lot to take in, mate." Otto was attempting to reassure him. "So, your grandad thinks that your spirit beast is a dragon?" His face lit up like a Christmas tree. "That's pretty epic, to be fair." Otto looked excited by the prospect of Arnold's spirit beast. "No one would mess with you again."

"I think my grandad was worried about me losing my temper. It sounds like that was what happened to my grandma."

"Need to keep a lid on it then, mate. Was there not a book up there about dragon spirit beasts? Maybe we can start there. Try and get some more information that will help us." He pointed over to the wall of books on the far side of the Athenaeum, indicating where he thought the book might be. "We have the ladders, remember. Perhaps we should use them this time," Otto joked.

The glass double doors at the entrance unfrosted and opened and Mr. Whitaker walked into the room. He did not look happy, but then it was no different from what they had become accustomed to. He was wearing a nice light grey suit with a white shirt and pink tie and he stood within the Athenaeum and began to straighten his cuffs as he spoke. "Please, can you both come this way." He spun on his highly polished shoes and set off to exit the Athenaeum. Looking at each other and gesturing for the other to go first, Otto decided to take the lead on this occasion and set off to follow Mr. Whitaker with Arnold just behind him.

Mr. Whitaker led them back into the main reception area for the Chichen and spun back on his heels again giving them both little time to adjust their speed and avoid clattering into him.

"How is your research?" There was a coldness to his voice that Arnold had not noticed the night of the Ch'ahb'. In fact, Mr. Whitaker had made them feel as though it was an inconvenience that they were there, even though it was him that insisted on them both joining. "You have had two months so far which seems to be a lot longer than usual for most candidates. I would like an update." He talked at them and not to them, rolling his eyes patronisingly which cemented the feeling for Arnold that Mr. Whitaker did not want them there. Otto stepped forward and raised his hand as if sarcastically saluting Mr. Whitaker.

"Sir, my spirit beast is definitely from the big cat family." Mr. Whitaker looked less than impressed with Otto's salute and stared at him until Otto lowered his arm.

"Two months to find that out? I could have told you that just from your auro totem in the Ch 'ahb'," he scolded. "Please tell me you have more than that, Master Redburn?" Mr. Whitaker looked less than impressed.

"Well with me becoming more athletic and stronger as well as showing characteristics such as loyalty, you know with still being friends with Arnold despite him not being able to keep up with me." Otto had mistaken confidence for cockiness now and he was most certainly coming across as overconfident. "That would leave me with options such as the panther, the leopard or the jaguar. If I had to hazard a guess, sir." Otto saluted towards Mr. Whitaker again as he signed off on his monologue. He looked across at Sue who was typing away at her desk and winked at her. She winked back at Otto which was the worst thing to do as he now had a crowd to play to. Mr. Whitaker's face darkened.

"Address me in such a patronising manner again, Master Redburn, and I will have you thrown out of this Chichen. If there is one trait I despise, it is that of overconfidence," he hissed, his tone of voice calm and unwavering. "Two months that has taken you. You have had the complete Athenaeum at your disposal, and this is all you have for me? I consider this a failure, a waste of your time and most certainly a waste of our resources." Mr. Whitaker did not look impressed at all.

"Mr. Whitaker, if I could-" Arnold started.

"I've heard enough already, Ethon," Mr. Whitaker said, cutting Arnold off straight away before he could go into detail on what he had discovered about himself. "I have heard enough with his half-hearted attempt at research and I am not prepared to listen to anymore." Arnold went to speak again but Mr. Whitaker held up his hand to stop him. "May I suggest that next time, you have more detailed answers for me before I have no choice but to reconsider your access to this and any other Chichen. You both have one week." He spun on his heels again and left them in the reception area just in front of Sue's desk.

"What an ass." Otto spoke first. He was used to acting the clown and certainly used to receiving such dressing downs. "One week? Does he realise I have done more reading in the last two months than I have in my entire life?" He placed his hands in his pockets. "I won't know what my spirit beast's true form is until It actually shows itself."

"It teaches discipline," said Sue, her soft voice drifting across to them. "It's not about how much information you can take in. It's about the discipline of following orders and persisting at your task."

"Waste of bloody time, if you ask me," Otto replied.

"Keep going. You're both doing really well. Regardless of what Mr. Whitaker says," she said, smiling at them both.

"Come on Otto, let's call it a night." Arnold set off towards the front door as he couldn't be bothered going back into the Athenaeum, feeling that it could wait until tomorrow. He had learned enough for one day.

"Boys," Sue called from behind her desk. The two of them turned around to see what Sue wanted. Arnold was beginning to feel hungry and wasn't so much as in the mood for idle chat. "Don't take it personally. He is like that with everyone. Some might say he has a stick up his, well, you know." She smiled at the two of them. Otto sniggered loud enough for it to echo through the reception area with Arnold quickly hushing him before Mr. Whitaker heard them. "Before you go, your dad is still in his office and he would like you both to go up and see him before you leave." The phone rang and Sue answered and began talking to the caller. Curious as to what they were wanted for they made their way up to his dad's office and knocked on the door.

"Come in." They opened the door and entered the dimly lit room. His dad looked as though he was just finishing up for the day as he shut his laptop.

"Ah, there you are. Come with me boys, there is something I want to show you." He moved from behind his desk and indicated for them to leave the office and followed them out. "Right this way." The joy on his face was clear to see; he seemed excited to show them something. They continued down the finely decorated corridor, the gold triangular pattern etched into the red carpets quickly passing them due to the pace that his dad was leading with. They reached the reception area and Arthur placed his finger on a pressure pad and a single door clicked indicating that it had been unlocked. "Not much further now," he grinned, as he held the door open and let the two of them pass him. "Keep going down this corridor to the bottom and then it's the last door on the right that we need." Arnold could feel himself becoming giddy with the apprehension of where they were going. He followed his dad's instructions and continued to the bottom of the corridor, passing a series of posh-looking vases that sat in different alcoves, as they made their way to their destination. Arnold was curious to where they were being led to and once he had reached the door he stood and waited for Otto and his dad to catch up, not realising how far ahead he had got. He stood there, eagerly waiting for them to join him and when they did, his dad placed his finger on another pressure pad door. The pressure pad beeped and he heard the door click as it unlocked. Unable to take the suspense any longer, Arnold pushed the door open and walked straight through, desperate to see what it was his dad had wanted to show them.

The large room was empty. It was bare, with nothing but mats lined up on the floor and around the walls as if creating a padded cell. Arnold couldn't help but feel underwhelmed at what had been revealed to them. He stood there momentarily with nothing but a light above him and felt hugely disappointed.

"This is where the next part of your training will begin," Arthur explained to them. Arnold wondered what the next stage would entail and was just about to speak when Otto jumped in first.

"I'm not being funny, Mr. Ethon, but if you are teaching us to dance, I'm out." He was laughing while talking as though he thought he was a stand-up comedian.

"As of right now, you will be coming to this room to complete your combat training. I want you to be able to at least defend yourself should the scarred man show his face again." His dad walked over to the side of the door and pressed his finger against another panel. There was a loud beep and over by the wall a panel slid to the side to reveal a doorway. "I have been waiting for your cast to come off, Arnold, before starting this part of your training. Please go and have a look."

"But the doctor said I had to rest," said Arnold, unconsciously holding his arm.

"I understand that, but we cannot wait any longer. You need to be able to defend yourself should he come back again." Arnold and Otto made their way to the opening to have a look at what was behind the panel, the smooth opening motion representing the high standard of technology that the Chichen used. Arnold stood at the opening and had no idea what to say. In front of them lay row upon row of every type of close combat weaponry imaginable. Swords glistened under the lights, the steel used for them polished so finely that Arnold would no doubt be able to see his reflection in them. There was a row of large spears each individually carved from the darkest wood that either of them had ever seen. To the side of the room, there was a rack containing different shields, each of different shapes and sizes with different animal hieroglyphs carved into them. As inspiring as the vast collection was, Arnold also felt incredibly daunted at the sight of such weaponry.

"We have to learn to use these?" Arnold asked, a concerned look on his face.

"Eventually," his dad replied, "You will need to train with wooden and blunted weapons first before you train with these. This is for your own safety."

"Do you think he will come back again?" Otto asked. "Do you even know where the scarred man is?"

Arthur walked over to the weapons room and picked up a spear. He began waving it around demonstrating how much he was accustomed to using it, moving with a fluidity and elegance that it was as if he was dancing with it. "We don't," he responded simply. "He disappears as easily as he appears, so we have no idea where he is and that concerns me." He began to spin the spear around his body and above his head before coming to an abrupt stop and standing straight with the spear stood beside him. "I need to make sure you are prepared physically for if he was to come back again. You were lucky last time, Arnold."

"You don't need to tell me, dad. If it wasn't for your spirit beast..." Arnold stopped talking, remembering how close he came to not being here now.

"It would be easier if we had our spirit beasts to protect us." Otto was becoming just as eager as Arnold in wanting to know what his spirit beast was.

"Well, unfortunately, you have not mastered your auro yet and you will have sessions around this too but in the meantime, sticks will have to do." There was a bluntness to Arthur's comments and from time to time he needed to be firm with the pair. This was one of those times. "I nearly lost you at the hospital because we were not prepared and I will not let that happen again."

Arnold's dad pulled two training swords from the rack and threw them towards Arnold and Otto. Arnold managed to catch his but was surprised by the weight which jolted his arm, causing it to ache slightly. He stood with the wooden sword, not knowing what stance to take so standing up straight with the hilt grasped tightly in his hand. Arthur began walking down the length of the training room with his hands behind his back. "First thing's first. A Doyen does not kill. We capture our opponents in battle and arrest them. This is our way. You must always remember this, no matter what. You must always keep control of your anger." He stopped and faced Arnold and Otto. "Now. I want you both to try and beat me." Arnold felt awkward as he had not had a playfight with his dad for years. "You want us to fight you with these? They're kind of heavy -" Before Arnold could continue, Otto charged at Arthur, letting out a sad attempt at a battle cry, swinging his wooden sword back and taking his shot. His dad simply stepped to the side and laughed, as Otto's momentum took him straight past Arthur and left him to crash against the wall.

"Your turn, Arnold," his dad said, smiling. Arnold still felt awkward and moved towards his dad with apprehension. As he reached him, he lamely stuck his wooden sword out to jab at him. His dad slapped the sword out of the way and pushed him back with both hands, with more force than Arnold expected. Arnold lost his footing and stumbled backward, before falling to the floor.

"You have to try harder than that, Arnold. The less effort you put in, the more I will push you back." Arthur stood over Arnold and offered him his outstretched his hand to help him to his feet. Arnold smiled back at his dad and decided he would up his game, knocking his dad's hand away and swinging the wooden sword straight at his legs. His dad simply lifted his leg up, meaning that Arnold's swing missed. He stepped back and smiled at him. "That's more like it! Now let's try again. Both of you try attacking me at the same time." He turned and winked at Otto who was still smarting from clattering into the wall. The two of them looked at each other and then ran towards his dad. Otto had raised his wooden sword behind his head, so Arnold did the same. They were on either side of him; Arnold to the front and Otto to the rear. They continued their run and swung their training weapons down at his dad with more force than the first time. Arthur stepped to the side again, watching the pair wince as the wooden swords came crashing down on each other's shoulders. Luckily for Arnold, this was on his left side and not on the side where he had just had his cast removed. His dad then turned and pushed with force again and they both fell sideways in a heap on the floor.

"Might take a while this," Otto chuckled while climbing back to his feet. "Ow." He glanced a look at Arnold, not exactly thankful for the blow he had just received.

"Same," Arnold replied, as he got back to his feet.

"This is why I need to train you. You are both clumsy and would not last two seconds in combat if he returned. I know I said that the Doyen way was to capture not kill, however, if he turns up again, I want you to be able to defend yourselves and run, do you understand me? You do not try and catch him. He is far stronger and will not hesitate to kill either of you." Arthur's seriousness was written all over his face. He was genuinely concerned that the scarred man was going to return. "Defend and run. DO NOT actively attack. This guy is trained and will play to your weaknesses." Arnold and Otto's loud panting stopped as they had gathered their breath. They stood side by side with their swords in hand, waiting for further instruction from

Arnold's dad.

"Right, let's work on that footwork first." His dad got another training sword from the weapons room and stood in front of them. "Each weapon requires different footwork that you need to use it as effectively as possible. For now, we will focus on the sword". He adapted his feet to show a way in which to place their feet; one foot pointing forward, one pointing to the side and slightly behind the other. "Copy my footwork," he instructed. As requested, the two put their feet in the position they had just been shown with their training swords awkwardly by their side. Arnold felt unbalanced by the sword and tried holding it in different ways to try and discover the most comfortable position.

"Try holding it the way you did when you tried to attack me," Arthur hinted, seeing that they were not going to figure this out for themselves. Lifting the weapon above his head, Arnold suddenly felt better balanced. He held his position, finding the stance more comfortable. Otto copied Arnold's position and looked equally relieved to now be standing in a less awkward position. "Hold that position. Now take a step forward with your left foot, bringing your right foot in behind. As you do, strike downwards with your weapon then return to your initial standing position." His dad showed an example of the move that he wanted them both complete. Arnold copied the steps slowly wanting to make sure that he got the combination right. Left foot, right foot, strike he thought to himself, talking through the steps to make sure it stuck. He looked to his side to see Otto complete the steps with ease. He knew that he would find it easier as he was a lot more athletic than Arnold. Arnold did what his dad asked and returned to his starting stance.

"Again," Arthur demanded. Arnold did as he was asked. "Again," Arthur repeated.

When they reached the far side of the training room they turned and went back up the hall the other way. They continued this for the next hour, patrolling the room and focusing on the footwork they had been shown. Arthur stood at the side of them shouting when they were to do their next step like a sergeant major drilling his troops. Arnold felt tired, his arms felt heavier than lead from holding the wooden sword over the top of his head for the last hour. His dad had been relentless and not allowed them to have a break. Arnold could feel the sweat on his face and had the thick taste of iron in his mouth. He didn't know how much longer he could continue with this. Both he and Otto had so far managed to keep up with the pace but even Otto, who was much more physically capable than Arnold, was beginning to show signs of fatigue. The throbbing in Arnold's right arm was tremendous and he felt as though he could feel his main vein pulsating as he continued to work through the move they had been shown. His throat felt dry and had begun to itch as he wished that the session would end so that he could get a much-needed drink.

"That's enough now boys. You can stop. Please put your weapons back in the rack." Arthur clapped and appeared happy at what he had just seen them both achieve. "Well done, take a drink and have five minutes." Arnold dragged himself to the weapons room to place his wooden sword on the rack. His legs felt like noodles and although walking normally still felt as though he was moving with his feet still in stance. His right arm continued to throb from the exertion with the weapon and he felt like his chest was going to implode, he had never done anything like this before and he felt drained of his energy.

Otto placed his sword on the rack and grinned. "That was great," he exclaimed, clearly feeling a lot more energised than Arnold was right now.

"How can you be feeling ok after that? I feel exhausted." Arnold could not believe how utterly relaxed Otto appeared.

"I feel great! Nothing like a good workout," he said, flexing his arm muscles. Arnold envied how easily Otto had adapted, no doubt because of his spirit beast. He wished he could be more like him. Arnold couldn't help the frustration that Otto was left feeling energised and he was left feeling like he was made out of marshmallows like all his bones had no structure to them anymore. He swallowed his frustrations, his throat still burning in desperation for a cold drink. He walked shakily to his bag and pulled out a bottle of juice he had brought, opened it and gulped it down. The sweet orange replaced the metallic iron taste that he had from overexerting himself with the gruelling training exercise.

"Same again, tomorrow." Otto grinned, his keenness for more training showing in his face. "We will be training physically three times a week from now on, with your rest days being spent in the Athenaeum and learning how to channel your auro." His dad was serious when he said they needed to train so that they could defend themselves. "I warned you at the beginning this was not going to be easy. Today was just a taste of what you will need to endure to truly hone your skills and abilities." There was a steeliness about his voice. Arnold put his drink in his bag. The metallic taste had now subsided, and his breathing was back to a steady rhythm. He pulled his t-shirt up to wipe the cold sweat that had collated on his forehead, leaving a wet patch on his shirt. He understood the reasoning for needing to train this hard, but it did not mean he enjoyed it one bit. He could only hope that with time it would get easier.

Chapter Seventeen

Arnold didn't really enjoy the next few weeks. The whispers and funny looks at school had settled down, however they had not completely stopped. He hated the fact that because he and Otto had been invited into the Chichen that most people at school had started being weird around them. Since the confrontation at school with Peter and his goons, they had left them alone for the most part. Peter would stare at Arnold as though he was still bearing a grudge from time to time, but it wasn't anything that Arnold didn't feel comfortable dealing with.

After school Arnold had been to the Chichen either to carry out more research in the Athenaeum or to be savaged in combat training by his dad. Otto had taken to it like a duck to water but Arnold was just not as fit as Otto and he was still feeling frustrated. What he would give just to be able to complete one training session and feel the energising buzz that Otto would drone on about at the end of each session. The good news for Arnold was that they had completed three training sessions this week which meant there were no more for a few days. Arnold looked forward to going to the Chichen this evening though as they would be honing a new skill, something that he was sure would enable him to gain a better understanding of his spirit beast. This evening they were learning how to channel their auro. More than ever Arnold wanted to feel better connected with his spirit beast and he was becoming increasingly anxious, feeling as though he was not developing as quickly as he should have been. Learning how to channel his auro was the best way he was going to discover his spirit beast, or at least he thought so.

After finishing school, Arnold had opted to walk to the Chichen by himself, telling Otto that he would meet him there. His jealousy over Otto taking to life at the Chichen better than him despite it being Arnold who had always wanted to join was beginning to show. Otto trained better than him, was stronger, faster and, at the moment, more eager. The perfect student.

He ruminated to himself as he approached the big oak door that he had become accustomed to at the entrance to the Chichen. He opened it and entered the reception area to find Otto already waiting for him so they could begin their training for the day. His eagerness irritated Arnold.

"Took your time," Otto quipped, his timing perfect as ever.

"We can't all be as perfect as you," Arnold sniped back. It was unusual for him to be so touchy, but he felt the resentment that was bubbling just under the surface. His words went straight over Otto's head though as he was oblivious to how Arnold was currently feeling.

"Take a seat, boys, your dad will be down in a moment," Sue said as pleasantly as usual, directing the boys to a row of chairs in the reception area. They walked across and sat in the chairs as directed by Sue, Arnold choosing to sit on the third seat to leave a gap between himself and Otto. Sitting there, he began to tap his foot on the floor, something he did when he was feeling stressed or anxious. Placing his hand on his knee he attempted to consciously stop himself from doing it. He had started off the evening really looking forward to this session but suddenly found that his irritation towards Otto meant he was now not in the mood at all.

Around five minutes passed without either speaking a word to each other as they waited for Arnold's dad to come and find them for their session. Arnold continued to look at the clock wondering what was taking him so long. Another ten minutes passed, and Arnold continued to look at the clock. He had already counted each individual chequered square on the floor in front of him to relieve his boredom. Arnold started tapping his hand on his knee now that he had stopped tapping his foot on the floor.

"Where is he?" Arnold muttered to himself. His dad was never this late to meet them when they needed to train.

"Not like your dad," Otto added, hearing Arnold speak to himself. "Should we just go to his office?" he asked, looking for guidance from Arnold.

"Sue told us to wait here," Arnold replied. "I think we are best doing as we're told."

"Your dad can't make it this evening. He's a little tied up with something right now," Mr. Whitaker announced as he walked around the corridor, his manner sharp and as unhospitable as you could imagine. "Your session this evening will be with me. I expect nothing but concentration from you both as I do not want to waste my precious time."

"This should be fun," Otto whispered. Arnold smiled for the first time this evening. He knew that Mr. Whitaker wasn't Otto's biggest fan which meant he might not excel with that extra pressure.

"This way! Keep up!" Mr. Whitaker set off in the direction of the training room, his body language closed and cold. They followed him down the usual corridor ending up at the training room and entered to begin their session. "Sit there." Mr. Whitaker pointed with his eyes, his hands arrogantly placed behind his back. Arnold and Otto sat on the floor waiting for Mr. Whitaker to begin. He closed the door to the training room and began the session. "I am informed that today you are to learn more about channelling your auro. This will test you mentally and physically so if you do not feel capable of keeping up you may stop at any time. I will not be walking you through this. I will be explaining the principles and it is up to you to ensure you follow my instructions. Do you both understand?" Mr. Whitaker was abrupt as usual. "I have far better things to do than be wasting my time here with you two."

"Yes Sir," they answered in unison.

"Your auro is what binds your spirit beast to yourself. It is what connects you to the spirit world. Channel this and you will become more in tune thus enabling you to have a greater connection with your spirit beast." Mr. Whitaker was walking slowly up and down the training room behind them, a calm manner about him now, his tone of voice softer than usual. "Some people have dreams like yourself Arnold, others can merely feel the presence of their spirit beast. This process will help you on your journey." He stopped pacing and picked up two small bottles from a table at the edge of the room. "Now drink this, close your eyes and listen to my voice." He handed them a bottle each.

Arnold accepted the bottle and drank from it quickly. It tasted bitter and left a nasty taste in the back of his throat as if he had just swallowed a load of flowers. He closed his eyes as directed, not really knowing what to do next. Otto did the same.

"Now I need you to think about one thing personal to you that you need guidance on then focus on that and nothing else. I need you to remain calm, keep your breathing steady and just stay focused." Mr. Whitaker continued to walk up and down the training room as he spoke. Arnold continued to draw slow, deep breaths and began to think about what he needed guidance on. More than anything he wanted to know that he had a spirit beast and he wanted to know what form it would take. He continued to focus on this while slowly inhaling and exhaling, his body feeling relaxed as he sat there in a semi meditative state. He continued with this until he found himself dreaming again. At least it felt like a dream, but Arnold also felt like he was still awake. It was a strange sensation like nothing Arnold had felt before. Arnold felt aware of his own consciousness, about his surroundings but yet was dreaming for the first time in a long time that he was flying again. He wasn't in the powerful body that he found himself occupying in his last dream and the surroundings were not the same as usual, however, it still seemed strangely familiar to Arnold. Soaring through the sky, Arnold did not feel in control but more like a passenger. He was looking through the eyes of the spirit beast but could not feel any of the other sensations that he had become accustomed to. He could still take in the amazing view, his breath was taken away once more like every other time he was this high up. Arnold continued to look out with that feeling of familiarity nagging at the back of his mind. Unable to shake this feeling, Arnold began to focus on the buildings that were whooshing past beneath him. Whereas in his other dreams he had been flying above hills, lakes, and mountains, this time he was flying over a town. He continued to look down below to see if he recognised any of the buildings and he spotted something; a large building which he felt as though he knew but couldn't quite put his finger on what it was. He wasn't in control of which direction he was flying in and this really frustrated him. He wished that they could fly down lower so that he could take a closer look at the building.

Suddenly his flight path changed, he felt himself lowering down closer to the building. Arnold suddenly felt more connected to the spirit beast. He swooped down just above the building to the point where he could recognise it clearly. It was the Civic Theatre that was just down the road from where he lived. The spirit beast was flying above Oswald. The flight path continued over the top of the theatre and he felt as though he was being drawn towards it like a magnet pulling the two together. Arnold realised that the spirit beast was heading in the direction of the Chichen. Excitement filled his head and he felt goosebumps all over his body, his hairs on his arms standing on edge. Arnold knew that his spirit beast was on its way to find him and he knew he was just about to find out its identity. He was about to connect with it. As the spirit swooped above Oswald, Arnold saw the Chichen and felt the pull towards it, feeling the pull in his physical body as it swooped down. Approaching the Chichen, the pull felt even stronger as though even if he wanted to, they wouldn't be able to pull away at this point.

Suddenly, Arnold fell to his side and was promptly brought back from his dream. Dazed and confused, he gathered his bearings before realising his spirit beast was nowhere to be seen. More than anything he felt infuriated that he had been stopped from what he was certain was him connecting with his spirit beast and couldn't understand how this would be taken away from him at the last possible second. Then again, he had become accustomed to the persistent knock backs and knockdowns and he honestly didn't know how much more of this he could take.

Gathering himself, Arnold sat himself back up and looked around the room which was still a bit of a blur as he had been in a deep meditative state whilst dreaming of his spirit beast. A soft glow was emitting from the room, one that Arnold instantly recognised as that from a spirit beast. Standing to his feet, he felt the happiness he had been searching for, for so long. This was short-lived as he soon realised that it was not his spirit beast stood before them in the training room; it was Otto's. His auro glowing brightly around him and his spirit beast. Otto had a joyous look on his face, a look of real pride, a look that Arnold craved so badly but again found himself disappointed.

Otto's smile ran from ear to ear. "It's a leopard!" he exclaimed, overjoyed at connecting his auro to his spirit beast.

"I do believe that is a Jaguar," Mr. Whitaker corrected. "Quite the rare spirit beast, Mr. Redburn. I'm sure your dad will be very proud." There was a hint of sarcasm in Mr. Whitaker's compliment.

The jaguar spirit beast sat calmly in front of Otto as they stared intently at each other as if taking in every tiny detail that they could at that moment. The jaguar's tail was not still and was moving around slowly behind where it sat, a sign of contentment. The soft glow around it made the dark dotted pattern on its body appear even more beautiful. Otto stepped towards the jaguar and placed his hand out towards it slowly, the jaguar nodded its head and lowered its crown allowing him to make contact.

"It feels warm," Otto grinned, as he placed his hand on the head of his spirit beast. Arnold felt the jealousy building up inside of him again and did not feel able to keep his thoughts to himself any longer.

"You just couldn't help it, could you?" Arnold spat, the anger distorting his features. "I was literally about to connect with my spirit beast when you knocked me over and broke my connection, and now here you are showing off with your own spirit beast instead." The venom in Arnold's voice was toxic; he'd had enough of being behind

Otto every step of the way and could not be bothered with it anymore. "I'm done with this, I'm done with all of it. I can't do this anymore!" Standing up he stormed across the room passing Mr. Whitaker along the way, shooting him a look of hatred.

"Eh?" Otto stood with his jaguar at the other end of the training room not understanding Arnold's outburst. He also looked hurt by what his close friend had just said to him.

Arnold charged out of the door nearly taking the frosted glass from its casing. He walked back down the corridor at pace, his head whirling from everything that had been going on recently as he made his way past reception.

"Arnold, are you ok?" Sue asked, obviously concerned but Arnold completely blanked her, choosing to focus entirely on the front door of the Chichén so that he could escape the confines of what felt like a prison. Nothing positive was happening here and he desperately wanted to be away from it. He slid open the door and stepped outside; it was dusk, and the sun was just beginning to set. An orange glow filled the sky making the clouds appear almost purple. Taking a deep breath of fresh air Arnold attempted to calm himself but he couldn't, he was far too angry. He could feel a rage building up inside of him that he did not have control of. Was this the dragon inside of him? He knew he needed to calm down and get control of his emotions.

Realising he needed to find a way to let off some steam Arnold set off at a pace, walking at speed as he hopped down the steps of the Chichen and continued down the street. He didn't know where he was going but just knew that he needed to shake off this anger that was currently consuming him. He continued with his fast walk but finding this unhelpful, set off at a jog. His anger was not subsiding, if anything it was getting worse. All he kept thinking about while running was how he was frustrated about Otto's progression while he was left to stagnate. Watching him get faster, stronger, better at combat and now getting to find out what his spirit beast was while Arnold was left behind. No matter how hard he tried Otto was always a few steps ahead and it was driving him mad. He was simply not developing like Otto and it wasn't fair.

As he continued his run, he lost his footing and felt himself slam against the ground, grazing his face and hands on the floor. Gathering himself he let out a loud scream, the rasp hitting him in the back of the throat, a result of his ever-building frustrations. This helped a little but did not stem the stinging sensation that had engulfed his face. Getting back to his feet and looking at the path behind him Arnold could not see anything that may have been the cause of his fall. He looked at his foot which had started to throb slightly realising that he must have tripped over something for his foot to be hurting so badly. Arnold looked back at the path again where he had fallen but there was nothing there that he could have tripped over. Arnold attempted to gather himself, he could hear the faint sound of distant cars and a dog barking as well as a ringing in his ears due to the collision with the floor. Confused, Arnold readied himself to set off running again but he didn't get a chance. He found himself knocked to the floor again. He attempted to look at who had knocked him over but as he spun around, he took a blow to the head and everything went dark. And just like that, his anger disappeared.

When he came to, everything around him was blurred and he instantly recognised the dull ache in his head like the mild concussion he'd suffered a few months earlier. The room was dark and there was a dampness in the air and a musty smell which when combined with his concussion made Arnold feel nauseous. He gazed around at his surroundings, but the lighting was limited in the room with only some rays of light coming in through the gaps in the boarded-up windows. A cloud of dust could be seen dancing around in the light with no set direction implying there were no open vents or windows.

Realising he was sat in a chair he attempted to stand up but found that he had been bound. Panicking, he attempted to shout out but realised that he also had been gagged, preventing him from calling for help. All he could muster was a muffled cry as the seriousness of his situation hit him. Tears began to roll down his face as he began crying, terrified about what might happen to him next. His eyes stinging and his cheeks wet from his tears, Arnold could feel the dust in the air sticking to his face like clingfilm. He struggled as hard and as frantic as he could to try and release himself from his constraints, but it was to no avail. His muffled cry for help fell on empty walls; no one was around to help him, no one was around to rescue him, and he had never felt so scared. Arnold's adrenaline was soaring and the fear that he was experiencing was consuming him. His body was trembling as he continued to try and look around for any clues as to where he was but was frustrated as he couldn't see enough of the room. The door to the side of him began to creak open and Arnold's heart continued to race at the thought of who it was who had done this to him. The shadow of a strongly built figure filled the doorway and Arnold instantly recognised who it was, his heart sinking in his chest. Stepping forward, a dust-filled ray of light confirmed his fears. It was the scarred man.

Arnold started struggling frantically again. He was scared before, but this revelation had magnified the terror by a thousand now. The constraints on his arms that bound them tightly to the chair where he was sat were digging into his skin but the fear consuming him meant that he didn't even notice the pain. The scarred man walked into the room slowly, the cement floor underneath his shoes echoing through the room. Stopping a few feet away from Arnold, he stood with his arms behind his back. The dust in the room hit the shafts of light making it seem like it was dancing around him. He stood staring at Arnold, only half of his scarred face visible due to the gloominess of the room.

Arnold looked at him, wanting to ask what he was going to do to him but all that came out was a muffled attempt at forming words, the tears still streaming down his face. He took a closer look at the man that had already caused so much anguish and chaos. The scars across the man's cheek were smooth but dominated the left side of his face. They ran over his eye, down past his lips in three almost symmetrical lines, the strange scarring indicating that this was done by a spirit beast.

The scarred man continued to fix his stare on Arnold, making him feel even more uncomfortable. Arnold averted his gaze to avoid eye contact with his captor, not through choice but through fear and intimidation. Arnold felt so weak and vulnerable and there was absolutely nothing he could do to help himself. He was at the mercy of the scarred man, a position that he never thought he would find himself in.

The man was breathing heavily, the look of fury etched across every inch of his face and his body. He continued to stare at Arnold for what felt like an eternity, each second that passed felt like much longer than it was. The scarred man's breathing began to steady to a slower rhythm, and he appeared in more control of his anger. His breaths were now deep and slow, and he turned and walked back out of the room without speaking a word to Arnold, the door creaking shut behind him.

Arnold stared at the door expecting the scarred man to come back in but after a short period of waiting, he was still alone. Feeling claustrophobic from being bound to the chair and having a gag in his mouth he began to sob uncontrollably, part in relief that the scarred man had left without hurting him and part from the confusion that he had not said a single word to him. He had not told him why he was here, why he had taken him or what he was going to do to him.

Arnold gathered himself by taking some deep breaths. He was petrified but sitting here crying was not going to help; he needed to try and be proactive. He had given up trying to pull his arms free, establishing that they were very much fastened to the chair and not going anywhere regardless of how hard he tried. He needed to focus his energy on something else. His feet were also bound to the legs of the chair meaning that he couldn't stand up or kick out. Arnold began to rock the chair from side to side which, to his surprise, worked so he kept on rocking his body against each side of the chair until eventually, he had enough momentum to fall over to the side. The chair clattered into the floor and Arnold instantly regretted his decision to do this as his head bounced off the floor because he was unable to brace himself with his arms tied down. Arnold could hear a strange ringing noise which he soon realised was due to the impact of his head on the floor and for a few moments, he felt as though his hearing was muffled from the impact.

Arnold pulled against his constraints to see if they had loosened and he found his right hand was slightly less restrained than it was before. He kept on pulling his right hand against the bindings, the material cutting into his skin, but he was determined to get his arm free, as he was desperate to escape this place before the scarred man came back. The friction burn on his arm was causing discomfort, but it was a pain that he could manage. He continued to manoeuvre his arm until eventually, he was able to create a gap big enough for him to slide his arm back and underneath the constraints, meaning he had an arm free! He then focussed on untying his other arm with his free arm which was much easier than trying to wrestle it free. Once he had done this he then moved onto freeing his legs.

After removing himself from the constraints, Arnold pulled himself up using the overturned chair and steadied himself, his concussion making him feel dizzy as he tried to get his bearings. Arnold began walking around the room looking for any form of a sign that would indicate where he was. He looked at the windows as a point of exit, but they were sealed on the outside with what looked like rusted metal sheets and planks of wood. The only way out was the single door the scarred man had entered and exited from just before. Arnold couldn't see clearly around the room and began to slowly walk across towards the door to the far side. He could hear his heartbeat and he felt wet on the side of his head. He raised his hand to touch his head and put his hand in front of a stream of light to reveal that he had cut his head and it was bleeding. His head was throbbing as he made his way to the battered door at the entrance to the room, he had no idea what he was going to do once he had got out of there, he just knew that he needed to try. Something felt off though, as much as he had injured himself breaking free from the chair this had been too easy. Surely, he must have heard the chair clatter to the floor, he thought to himself. He reached for the door to find that it wasn't locked so he pulled it open towards him, the creaking noise making Arnold's heart race fast again. The darkness in the room was unforgiving and created a very creepy environment.

The door opened and Arnold staggered backwards in horror; the scarred man had been stood behind the door listening to him this entire time, teasing, letting Arnold feel as though he had a slither of hope to escape and then cruelly snatching that hope away from him.

"You're not getting out that easily," he hissed. Arnold stared up from the floor, the fear flooding back, not that it had really subsided in the first place. Arnold had no idea what the scarred man wanted with him, but he was sure that he was just about to find out.

Chapter Eighteen

Otto stood opened mouth, not fully understanding the outburst that he had just been subjected to. Feeling confused and a little hurt by what Arnold had just said to him, he shook his head in disbelief. He had just managed to summon his spirit beast for the first time, and it should have been a happy experience, yet he was being made to feel guilty for doing it. All he really wanted at that moment was for his best friend to be happy for him, but it felt as if it wasn't the Arnold show then his so-called best friend was not interested, which had hurt him deeply.

"What the hell was that?" he called out, seeking some form of reassurance from Mr. Whitaker even though he knew that it wouldn't be forthcoming. Mr. Whitaker didn't say anything as Otto had predicted, his silence bringing an even greater sense of awkwardness to the room.

"I suggest you find him, Redburn. It is in everyone's interest that Ethon remains calm." Otto wasn't vaguely interested in being careful and exited the room as instructed to find Arnold, not to calm him as instructed, but so he could have it out with him. Otto couldn't believe how much Arnold had been becoming more and more self-absorbed and selfish and he felt that he needed this pointing out before he pushed everyone away.

Otto stood in the corridor wondering momentarily where he might have gone. Looking down the hall he thought that Mr. Ethon's office might be a good place to start as Arnold may have gone to see him. Setting off, Otto made his way to the office, wondering what he was going to actually say to Arnold when he came face to face with him again. Reaching the office, he noticed that the door was slightly ajar and thinking that Arnold might be in there blowing off some steam, Otto followed. He walked up to the door slowly, listening out for Arnold ranting, but he couldn't hear him. All he could hear was a muffled sound, as though someone was talking but that they were being restricted. Peeking around the door, he discovered Arthur was tied to a chair with his mouth gagged, preventing him from calling out for help. He also had a swollen eye indicating that he had received a heavy blow to the face at some point.

Otto burst into the room "Are you ok? Who did this?" He moved behind Arthur and began to untie the rope that bound him. The rope was thick making it difficult, but he managed.

"What's going on here?" Otto's dark eyes shot up to see Mr. Whitaker stood in the doorway, staring straight at him and Arthur.

"You! You did this!" Otto roared. "You said he was tied up with work." Without thinking, Otto stepped to the side to create a clear path between himself and Mr. Whitaker and before he had time to think, he found himself running straight towards him at speed. Unable to control the rage he was feeling he used his momentum to throw himself at Mr. Whitaker and speared him with his shoulder. Mr. Whitaker let out a gasp of air as he was instantly winded. He attempted to keep his footing, but Otto's speed had caught him by surprise. They both fell backwards and clattered into the wall behind. Mr. Whitaker hit his head before the two hit the ground and as Otto recovered himself it soon became apparent that he was unconscious. Otto stood back up and brushed himself down, turning around and running back to Arthur to untie him. Making persistent muffled sounds, Otto took this as Arthur wanting the gag to be removed so he could talk again. Otto grabbed the gag and pulled it downwards enabling him to breathe and talk freely.

"It's not Mr. Whitaker," Arthur gasped, "he has nothing to do with this."

"Then who did this to you?" Otto replied, completely confused.

"Sue."

"Sue did this? But why?" Otto frowned.

"She is working with the scarred man and she has been this whole time. Feeding him information." Arthur explained as Otto began loosening the bindings. "Where's Arnold, is he ok?"

"He had a blow out with me and stormed off. I came here looking for him," Otto explained, starting to become more concerned for his best friend's safety than having it out with him.

"We need to find him. They want to make him angry. They want him to release his dragon."

"Er, he was pretty angry when he left me," Otto said, as he finished untying Arthur. The two of them exited the Chichen as fast as they could, looking to find Arnold and make sure that he was ok. Their concern growing, they looked at the darkened area outside and could not see any sign of him. Running down the steps they continued to look around with Arthur's worry becoming more and more evident on his drawn face.

Pulling out his phone, Arthur began to ring his wife to see if she had heard from him, however, the phone rang out adding to his growing fears for his son's safety. "We need to head home and see if he has gone there. My car is down here, come on." Otto followed Arthur and the two of them got in the car as fast as they could. Turning on the engine, Arthur's wheels span on the spot momentarily before the tyres let out a loud screeching noise and they accelerated quickly down the road.

Pulling up outside the house they could see that the lights were on and the curtains remained open. Arnold's grandad could be seen in the window smiling as he stood talking to his mum. They clambered out of the car and ran to the house, bursting through the door.

"Arnold!" Arthur shouted his voice broken and cracked. "Arnold, are you here?" He moved to the bottom of the stairs as he shouted up them hoping for a response that would allay his fears.

"What is going on? Why are you shouting?" Eve walked out into the hallway looking perplexed. "Arthur, what happened to your eye?"

"It's Arnold, I don't know where he is, have you seen him?" Arthur replied, panic obvious in his voice. "It's Sue! She's been working with the scarred man this whole time and I think I know why they would want Arnold...we need to find him. We need to stop them, Eve."

"They have Arnold?" His grandad said, entering the hall to quiz him further. "Where?"

"I don't know where he could be. We never found any clues as to where the scarred man disappeared to after he murdered Charles." Otto looked at the adults in front of him and began to feel confused as to why anyone would take Arnold. Listening to the adults talk, Otto looked around for anything that might help them find his friend and he noticed Arnold's note pad placed on the small table in the hall.

"The tower!" It was turned to the page containing the drawing of the tower that he had told Otto about. "Could that be of any help?" Otto pointed at the pad to draw everyone else's attention to it.

"No, I already told him that I did not recognise the tower," Arthur dismissed.

"Let me have a look." Arnold's grandad said as he walked across to the detailed drawing. Picking up the pad he took a closer look at the sketch. "It can't be!" he gasped. "I know where this is Arthur - it's too much of a coincidence. This is where we did it, where we trapped her."

"There's a tower there?" Arthur quizzed, unaware that such a thing existed.

"It's overgrown and in a restricted area, with good reason. This is a place where there are increased energy levels that are linked directly to the spirit world. Not many people know about it. After what happened there, an Elder decreed that the ground wasn't safe because of damage caused by the mines and we quarantined the area."

"Then, how do you-" Otto began.

"Because I used to be an Elder, and it was me that sealed that place up a long time ago." Arnold's grandad tore the page from the notebook and placed it in his pocket. "We need to go right now, Arthur." The two of them made for the front door.

"I'll stay here in case Arnold turns up," Eve said. Otto began to follow as they left the front door.

"What are you doing?" Arnold's grandad asked, a stern look across his face.

"I want to help find him," He replied with an equally assertive, steely look.

"It's fine dad, he has been completing his training, the more help we have the better." The three of them moved towards the car at a fast pace and jumped into the vehicle.

"Stop at my house first, I need to pick something up," Arnold's grandad requested.

They set off down the road and within a couple of minutes, they were outside his house. Quickly exiting the car, Arnold's grandad ran inside and returned a few minutes later with something strapped to his back and holding some items in his hands. Otto squinted but could not make out what it was due to the darkness surrounding them. He walked around the back of the car and opened the boot before placing the items inside and closing it with a thud.

"It's been a while dad. You sure you remember how to use that thing?"

"Using a macahuitl is like riding a bike," he smiled. "Now let's go get my grandson back. I'll direct you to where we need to go, and I will get us up to the tower once we are there." Arthur set off as fast as he could down the road, taking each corner at speed, pushing the vehicle to its mechanical limits as he aimed to get to their target destination as quickly as possible. The three of them remained silent during their journey; Otto because he did not know what to say, the other two because they were trying to focus on what was ahead of them. Otto looked in the rear-view mirror and could see the worry in Arthur's eyes. He had never seen him like this before and it was hard to see someone who was clearly scared about what they were getting into.

After around twenty minutes of driving which could only be comparable to something Colin McRae would have been proud of, they arrived at a heavily wooded area. As soon as the car stopped the three of them climbed out and Otto stared into the vast darkness, unable to see past the trees that were in front of them. He could hear owls talking to each other and a slight rustling coming from the bushes which he presumed were either squirrels or a fox. Arthur and Arnold's grandad walked around to the back of the car and opened up the boot.

"Quite the collection." Arthur looked impressed by the variety of weapons that his dad had amassed and hoarded in his loft.

"Here - thought you would like this." He reached in and passed him a small spear.

"My old ceremonial spear! As if you still have this!" Taking hold of it, Arthur twisted it around halfway down and extended it, so it increased to a much more intimidating size. "Like riding a bike," he smiled.

"Otto take this." Arnold's grandad reached into the boot and pulled out an oval-shaped shield made of a darkened wood and decorated with various carvings of different animals. "I don't feel comfortable giving you a weapon, but at least you will be able to protect yourself." He passed the shield to Otto who had the look of a child at Christmas as he accepted it. Otto took the shield and was initially surprised by the weight of it, the wood was much heavier than it looked. Otto couldn't help but notice the faint smell of burnt cedar. It looked really old and Otto silently felt that it should really be in a museum somewhere rather than in his inexperienced hands. Placing his forearm through the straps on the inside of the shield offered slightly more comfort for Otto as he pulled the shield in front of him, waiting for instructions on what the next move was.

"Will this work? It seems pretty old."

"You will be fine with it," Arnold's grandad reassured him. "Do you have a torch, Arthur?"

"We don't need one." He began to wave his hands around and within a few seconds, his Bear had been summoned in front of him, its white glow illuminating the surrounding area and making the pathway increasingly visible for them.

"This way." Arnold's grandad led the trio and began to walk the path in front of them, the Bear spirit beast following closely behind, continuing to light up the surrounding area.

The light being emitted by the bear did not look like what you would see from a torch but more like natural daylight. It was a strange sight to behold and Otto couldn't take his eyes off it. He could feel his heart rate increasing as his increased nerves and adrenaline began to take hold. He could feel his arms trembling as he crept along the path, not knowing what was lying ahead of them. They continued to navigate the path, slowly making their way through the perpetual darkness with each step moving closer to Arnold.

Stopping suddenly, Arnold's grandad veered off the path and began to walk through some bushes before reaching some metal fencing. "Through here. We are not that far away now." He peeled back the corner to create a small opening and gestured for Otto and Arthur to crawl through. Otto removed his shield from his arm and slid this through before following it and replacing his arm through the tight leather straps on the back of it. Once everyone was through Otto stared at the bear wondering how such a large spirit beast would get through the small gap. He did not have to wonder for long as the bear walked up to the fence and began to pass through it as though it wasn't there at all.

"Can I help you?" The voice came from the side of them making Arnold's grandad instinctively lift his hand up to the hilt of the macahuitl that was strapped to his back. He did not recognise the voice, but Otto and Arthur did. It was the unmistakable softly spoken, reassuring voice of Sue the receptionist from the Chichen. Otto could not believe she was working with the scarred man after she had been so helpful and reassuring to both he and Arnold.

"Why Sue? Why would you do this?" Arthur asked aggressively, his teeth gritted as he waited for answers from his now, very much ex-colleague.

"Do you have any idea what it is like to be a menial?" Sue growled back.

"Sue-"

"Don't call me that. My name is Kiria," she said, stepping out from the shadows and into the light being provided by the spectral bear.

She looked completely different from what they were used to and she appeared to be wearing some type of body armour. It looked almost like a dress but still allowed her to move with ease and without restriction. "You have no idea what it is like to be laughed at and tormented throughout school, being looked at like you have leprosy by your so-called friends. Ending up alone with only yourself for company and all because I am unable to summon a spirit beast." She lowered her hands to her side, her look menacing, almost like a tiger ready to pounce at any moment. "He has shown me, he has trained me."

"Shown you? What do you mean?" Otto shouted back at her. "Where is Arnold?"

"He has shown me how to take someone else's spirit beast. He has even transferred some of his power into this dagger to help me do it." Lifting up her hand, she revealed a small blade tucked into a holster on the side of her leg. Her smile was becoming more menacing than before as she removed the blade and held it tightly in her hand. Otto was taken aback at how different Sue looked, so far from the polite, warm woman he had become accustomed to greeting them when they entered the Chichen. The woman before them was like an ice queen, cold, stony-faced and aggressive; it was as though it was a completely different person stood in front of them. Sue began to focus less on them and more on Arthur's grizzly bear spirit beast that was helping to keep the immediate area illuminated.

"That's not going to happen," Otto said, moving into the path of Sue's menacing gaze.

"Try and stop me," She scoffed.

"Dad, you go on. We will deal with Sue. You need to find Arnold, bring him home."

"Deal with me? DEAL WITH ME?" Her anger was taking over and she was losing her cool edge. "You have no idea what I am capable of, what he has taught me." She ran at Arthur and jumped through the air landing a dropkick straight to his chest sending him flying backwards into the muddied path behind him. Landing on the floor on her back, Sue instantly jumped back to her feet with the presence and agility of a gymnast. Otto saw Arnold's grandad head down the overgrown path behind her and disappear into the darkness, in pursuit of his friend. Before he had time to think, Sue was running towards him and aimed a powerful kick right at him. Instinctively, he lifted the shield which took most of the force, just managing to brace himself to stop from falling over.

Following on from her kick Sue swung her fist forward quickly, Otto this time not reacting fast enough, and the punch connected with Otto's cheek with a loud crunch. Otto was surprised by the force of the punch. Sue's power had surprised him as she seemed a lot stronger than her physical presence suggested. Sue continued her volley of assaults on Otto, a flurry of punches and kicks, the speed of which again took Otto by surprise. Each ferocious hit connected with him in his face, chest, and leg. Sue finished with another blow to Otto's face that sent him crashing to the floor.

Climbing back to his feet with determination, Otto took a step forward towards Sue but was overtaken by Arthur who flew past him, throwing a knee at Sue. She was able to block this and knock him away, but he had pre-empted this and extended his spear, swinging it in the opposite way that he was moving. Sue raised a hand to knock it away before stepping back and pulling out her twin daggers.

"I want your bear," she laughed maniacally, as though this was a game. Her mask was well and truly off.

"How is that even possible, Sue? You're not thinking clearly. He has corrupted you."

"Corrupted me?" She paused momentarily. "He saved me. When I was alone, he was there for me."

She launched herself at Arthur and began to stab at him with her daggers, the two of them dancing around each other and neither was holding back. They blocked each other's blows whilst both attempted to wound the other. Arthur lunged forward with his spear, but Sue stepped to the side and rolled into him, connecting her elbow into his sternum which caused him to stagger back.

Otto jumped in at this stage and opted to use his shield offensively, hammering the end of the shield into her midriff and knocking her back in return. She did not appreciate this and swung an arm up in his direction with Otto just managing to raise the shield to protect his face. Her dagger slammed into the shield and got stuck in the wood, such was the force that she was capable of. Sensing an opportunity, Otto dropped to the floor and swung a leg out, taking Sue's out in the process, her ribs making a cracking noise as she slammed into the floor. Jumping back to his feet again, Otto stood over Sue, frustrated and angry at how she could betray them in the manner that she had.

"How could you do this to us?" he yelled, beginning to lose control. He had never felt this angry before. Raising his shield above his head he looked down at Sue who grinned back at him, looking almost psychotic. Otto began to drop his shield towards Sue's head with as much force as he could muster but before it had the chance to connect, he found himself slammed to the floor.

"No!" Arthur shouted. "That is not our way. Capture not kill!" Otto sat up, angry he had been stopped from finishing her.

"But she deserves it! The deceit and the lies-"

"Capture Otto, no matter what. This is the path we take. Never take a life."

"You are both so weak." Sue winced as she attempted to sit up, but she clearly broke her ribs when she had been slammed against the floor. Turning around, Arthur slammed the hilt of his spear at her head, knocking her instantly unconscious. "We need to get to Arnold."

"What about her?" Otto asked. He could still feel the anger inside him but felt he was able to control it. "I'll keep an eye on her, you go and find him." Otto sat on a tree stump a couple of metres away from where Sue lay unconscious.

"Are you ok?" Arthur pressed.

"I'm fine," he said. "I just lost my cool. I'm ok now." Otto pressed his shield into the ground and then leaned against it, all the while fixing his gaze on Sue. "She's not going anywhere." Arthur nodded and disappeared into the darkness as he followed in the direction that Arnold's grandad had headed moments earlier, his spirit beast following close behind.

Otto continued to stare at Sue, the only light now from the crescent moon above them. He was so annoyed at what she had done to them and at what she had been hiding from them all along.

Sue let out a groan as she began to come around from her unconsciousness. She looked around and soon realised that it was just her and Otto. She attempted to shimmy herself up, this time using the tree that was directly behind her to help sit upright. "I see that anger inside you, that rage. I've never seen any signs of that in all your time at the Chichen."

"Shut up." Otto wasn't interested in what she had to say; he had lost all respect for her.

"Bit of a personality change. You've done it, haven't you? You've connected with it and know how to summon it. You have your spirit beast." Sue's eyes lit up when she realised what had changed about him.

"I said shut up!" Otto shouted, his body language beginning to mirror his mood.

"I want to see it. What is it? I am intrigued." Sue began to talk in an almost flirtatious manner as she tried to encourage Otto to play along with her, all the while having one of her daggers firmly planted in her hand behind her back. She had her plan and all she needed to do was to get Otto to play right into her hands. "You know the old man deserved it," she purred, "He isn't a bad person. He just wants revenge against those that wronged him. That's fair enough, surely?" Otto was trying his hardest to ignore her but could feel his anger rising once more. He closed his eyes momentarily and began to take some deep breaths. "He could help you too, make you stronger than you could possibly imagine-"

"I SAID SHUT UP!" Otto yelled. He had lost control of his anger and without trying, his spirit beast formed in front of him, the soft glow lighting up their immediate area. The intricate pattern of the jaguar's spots was like something you would see in an abstract painting. The spirit beast looked at Otto and then crouched down onto the floor. Otto was focusing on Sue, so consumed by rage at what she had done that he had not even acknowledged that his spirit beast was there. To Otto it was just Sue and himself, his focused stare firmly on her and all he wanted was for her to be gone. To Otto, she didn't deserve to be allowed to rot in jail especially if anything had happened to Arnold.

"He hates you, you know. I mean why would he like you? You have upstaged him every step of the way. Made him feel like he's in your shadow." She smiled at Otto. "You know the saying - with friends like you, who needs enemies. Well, soon he won't be around to be a friend to anyone."

His jaguar spirit beast began to crawl towards her, still crouched and ready to pounce at any moment. Sharing Otto's intense stare, it continued to move towards her with intent and purpose. It knew what it was going to do.

"Wh-what are you doing Otto?" Sue began to panic. "Make it stop, it's going to hurt me." Otto was oblivious to what Sue was saying; he was blinded by rage and not aware that his spirit beast was creeping towards her. As the spirit beast got close it paused for a moment, as if teasing its prey before jumping towards her. Sue swung the dagger from behind her and the beast roared as she buried the blade deep into its side. Otto let out a scream as he felt an excruciating pain tear through his ribs. "Stupid boy," she gloated. "Did you think that it would be that easy?" She twisted the blade to the side causing Otto and his spirit beast to wince. "I told you. He has shown me how to steal someone else's spirit beast and now I am going to steal yours. I will finally have one." The dagger began to glow, and Otto suddenly felt weak. He felt as though the energy was being drained from him. His spirit beast began to dissipate with its spectral energy being absorbed by the blade that was embedded in its side. Otto began to panic; he could see his newfound spirit beast fading away in front of him and he felt powerless to stop it. Using what energy he had remaining, he lifted his shield from the ground and launched it at Sue with as much force as he could muster. He heard a crack and a snap as it connected with Sue's head and she hit the floor with a sickening thud. The blade stopped glowing and his spirit beast began to reappear, his fatigue disappearing instantly. Otto walked over to Sue and saw that her neck was shaped in an unnatural position and he knew straight away that he had killed her. That had never been his intention at all, but he had lost his temper. His breathing was heavy, and he began to panic about what he had done. He had taken someone's life, something that was forbidden within the Chichen.

His spirit beast lay on its side, it's breathing laboured due to the knife that was still planted firmly in its side. It was making a low grumbling noise indicating it was in pain; Otto knew this as he still had a dull pain in the lower part of his ribs. Walking across he knelt next to the jaguar and placed his hand on its head to reassure it. With his other hand, he grabbed hold of the hilt of the blade and began to pull this from its side. The spirit beast let out a yelp due to the discomfort. The blade felt strange though and Otto could feel the energy in it as it pulsated up through his arm from the hilt. The pulsating wave began to intensify all the way to his shoulder until eventually, he could feel this strange energy throughout his body. Otto tried to let go of the blade, but he couldn't. It was almost like the energy coming from the blade was keeping his hand wrapped around it. The energy coursing through his body was as intense as it was overpowering. He dropped to his knees, unable to stand any longer and then let out an almighty scream. He was hurting everywhere, and he didn't know how to make it stop. His scream echoed through the thick woodlands and only stopped as Otto collapsed on the floor, the pain stopping as he fell into unconsciousness.

Chapter Nineteen

"Sit down," the scarred man snarled. This was less a request and more of a demand that Arnold needed to comply with. "I've been wanting to sit with you ever since our paths first crossed. It's a funny thing, fate." His frame filled the doorway, his persona matching the darkness that filled the room. Seeing little other option other than to do as requested, Arnold shuffled back towards the chair, picking it up and then sitting down.

"What do you-"

"Silence!" the scarred man interrupted, infuriated at Arnold's petulance. "You will only speak when I say it is ok to do so, do you understand? There's a lot to go through, a lot to learn and a lot to do." He stepped in from the door frame and stood in front of Arnold, blocking any light that could come from outside. "Try and escape and I will kill you. Try and sucker punch me and I will kill you. Nod if you understand." Arnold nodded furiously. The scarred man was intimidating enough, but he had already had a run-in with his lions before now and he did not want to come across them again.

A disturbing silence fell. All that could be heard was the aggressive breathing of the scarred man and the panicked breathing of Arnold. After a few seconds pause the scarred man continued. "That day when you stopped me from killing that coward. What if I told you that I am not the bad guy in all this? That it is all a matter of perception?"

"What do you-" Arnold started.

"Don't answer unless I tell you to, boy!" The scarred man slammed his fist against Arnold's leg with an incredible amount of force, his cracked face contorting with rage. Arnold's face drained. He had an instant dead leg which was now throbbing along with his head. He shouldn't have said anything, after all, that's what he was told to do, just sit and listen, but he had genuinely thought the scarred man had paused to wait for an answer. He wasn't going to make that mistake again. Arnold stared at the scarred man intently and simply nodded again to indicate that he understood.

"There are two paths we can take here. One where you listen to what I have to offer and maybe live to see another day and the other involves you meeting a slow, painful end. I suggest you choose wisely." His voice rasped with his barely disguised rage. "We are going to find out where your loyalties lie."

Arnold wasn't quite sure what the scarred man was talking about, but he opted to keep quiet rather than receive another blow. "You think it's so black and white, that I am the bad guy but that really is not the case. You will come to see things the way that I do. At first, I didn't realise who you were but now? Now I know who you are, and I know what you are capable of." The scarred man continued to prowl the room whilst continuing to speak "I'm not from this world you see. Well, I wasn't born here." Arnold was puzzled by this statement but decided to wait for the scarred man to explain rather than ask a question and risk losing a body part. "See I am a rarity. One of a kind - there is no one else like me. I was born in the spirit world." Arnold frowned at his captor but remained silent. "As I grew up, I soon found I could switch between here and the spirit world, except initially I had no control over where I would appear in this world. This did present some, let's call them, challenges. As I came of age, I came to the realisation that I did not have a spirit beast connected to me. So, I decided I needed to find a way to get one. You know, so I could exact my vengeance on those responsible for me being bound to the spirit world without a spirit beast to guide me." He stopped next to a rusted panel that covered one of the many windows in the room and slammed his hand against it, the force echoing through the derelict room and prompting Arnold to sit bolt upright. "I wanted to make everyone responsible pay for their role in what happened to me and my mum."

Pulling another chair across, the scarred man sat down opposite Arnold, his voice not as aggressive as before. "Then she explained to me about the dagger and its ability to bind spirit beasts to it and I knew I had to have it. This was my opportunity to have a spirit beast and become more powerful. She wouldn't let me have it though, not until I proved myself to her." Pulling the blade out he looked at each side of it, awestruck at its appearance and the workmanship that must have gone into crafting it. "It took me many years to earn this, Arnold. In that time, I managed to build a bit of a following whenever I was in this world. People who were amazed at my connection to the spirit world, menials who had no spirit beast connection and I offered to help. Some may say it's a cult, but the most important thing is nobody knows about us. Well, up until now." He leaned forward and whispered. "I have people everywhere, Arnold." Placing the blade back inside his overcoat he continued to talk normally. "I know how you have struggled with connecting with your spirit beast. I know the frustrations you must be feeling because I have been there. I can help you, Arnold. I can be the catalyst, the final piece of the puzzle for you. I can connect you to your spirit beast."

Arnold was intrigued but confused at the same time. If he wanted to help him why had he kidnapped him and tied him up? He was so desperate to have his spirit beast though and found himself genuinely interested in what the scarred man was saying to him. Arnold's previous encounters with the man remained in his head but his curiosity about what he was offering him pushed them to the back in his mind. Deep down he knew he had to do whatever it took to survive and look at what options lay before him; if he got his spirit beast along the way that would be a bonus.

"This is where my story started." The scarred man explained, dramatically spreading his arms and turning around. His aggressive tone was now replaced by an alarmingly charming manner. "It can be where yours does too. You see, there is a powerful link between this world and the spirit world right here in this tower." Walking towards Arnold he calmly pointed to a tree by the side. "I am going to tie you up again. I assure you that if you let me do this, then through the link here in this very building I will be able to connect you with your spirit beast. No more waiting, no more frustrations. What do you say?" Arnold's mouth was dry through slight dehydration, but he nodded, not really seeing what option he really had and feeling that the scarred man would simply do this with force if he did not agree. He walked over and sat down in the chair as the scarred man instructed. Arnold watched as the scarred man walked across the room, picked up the rope and began to bind him to the chair. The rope dug into his arms and side; there was no escaping from this.

"What now?" he asked curiously.

"We wait."

Tired and weary Arnold sat bound to the chair, his body aching. He just wanted to be back home, to be safe. He wanted to know what they were waiting for. Arnold's blood ran cold as he suddenly heard a loud scream from not so far away from where they were. It was spine chilling and Arnold could almost feel the pain that the person must have experienced for that kind of cry. Arnold's heart raced as he began to panic. Was that someone he knew?

The scarred man heard it too and the sinister smile returned to his face. He stood waiting, staring intently at the entrance to the room as if waiting for someone to arrive. Arnold also looked, wondering who the scarred man was waiting for. He heard some muffled shouting from outside and thought he recognised the voice. A metal door scraped against the ground as it was opened, and hurried footsteps grew ever louder. To Arnold's surprise, his grandad appeared out of the darkness of the doorway. "Grandad!" he shouted.

His grandad's attention was drawn straight away to Arnold tied to the chair "Arnold!" he called back while making his way across the room.

"Ah, ah, aaaah," The scarred man said, wagging his finger. "I'm not finished with him, yet." His demeanour completely changed in an instant and his barely controlled aggression returned. "I am helping him."

"What do you want?" his grandad demanded.

"You, then him or should I say, his spirit beast." He turned, pulling his overcoat to the side and pulling out his blade. It began to glow. Waving his hands around, he began to summon the spirit beasts using the blade. The two lions appeared in front of him, their eyes firmly fixed on their prey.

Arnold began to panic, there was nothing he could do to help his grandad who was old and no match for the lions. Arnold had personal experience with them and he had only just survived.

"Run!" he screamed, terrified at what was going to happen to his grandad but absolutely powerless to do anything to help. He could feel his frustration building to anger as he desperately tried to get free from the chair. His grandad turned from Arnold to face the scarred man and the lions.

"The Lions of Tsavo. I see that you have found a way to release them from the blade." Beginning to motion with his hands, Arnold knew instantly what his grandad was doing; he was summoning his spirit beast. A faint glow began to emit from his grandad and an animal took form in front of him. It was an Elk. Its large intimidating antlers protruded from its head as it turned to look at Arnold's grandad before turning back to face the lions. His grandad put his hand behind his back and took hold of his macahuitl. "I am here to take my grandson back, whatever it takes." The scarred man cracked a wicked smile.

"Very well." He raised a hand and the two lions began to run at Arnold's grandad. The elk ran towards one of the lions and lowered its head, clattering into it head on. Letting out a deafening roar the lion bounced across the ground, eventually sliding to a stop. The second lion ran past the elk directly at Arnold's grandad who was stood there calmly holding his macahuitl blade in both hands. The lion roared as it flew through the air with its paws outstretched, ready to strike the fatal blow.

"Grandad!" Arnold called out as loud as he could, sure he was about to lose him. His grandad continued to stand there calmly as the lion approached through the air. At the last possible second, he raised his macahuitl and brought it down against the lion's head. It made contact with such force that it was detached instantaneously from the rest of its body which came crashing down to the ground and slid to a motionless stop against the cold stone wall. The remaining lion let out a roar for its fallen brother and swiped at the elk making contact with its side.

The scarred man looked furious at what had just happened and how easily Arnold's grandad had defeated one of his lions. "How dare you," he growled. "Never mind. I will have a replacement soon enough." He charged down towards Arnold's grandad, raising his blade above his head, ready to plunge it into him but his grandad was able to knock it away with his macahuitl. The two of them began trading blows with each able to block the other's attacks simultaneously. Behind them, the elk and the lion continued to grapple with each other, the elk using its ginormous horns to keep the lion at bay and preventing it from being able to pounce.

Arnold remained bound to the chair, unable to move and unable to help his grandad. He could feel his frustrations continuing to build and wanted to help him before it was too late. He could see and was impressed at how his grandad was holding his own against the scarred man. It was as if he was still in his prime and not an elderly man at all. He watched as the scarred man repeatedly tried to make contact with his grandad, but he was fast enough to either dodge or block his attacks. The two of them continued with another flurry of attacks before pushing away from each other and pausing for a moment, the two of them breathing heavily and tiring from the exchange.

"Not bad old man, but we need to move things along." He charged at Arnold's grandad once more and the two of them connected their weapons and began to press against one another to get the upper hand.

"How does it feel to be back here after all this time?" the scarred man hissed through gritted teeth. "This is where you trapped her in the spirit world."

The colour drained from his grandad's face and he momentarily lost his concentration, and this is what the scared man was waiting for.

"How do you-" Before he had the chance to say another word, the scarred man knocked his macahuitl up into the air, spun and planted his blade into Arnold's grandad's side.

Everything from then on seemed to happen in slow motion. Arnold began to scream but no noise left his mouth. This couldn't be happening. He couldn't lose his grandad, not like this. He needed to get to him, and Arnold began frantically pushing against his bindings, but the thick ropes kept Arnold firmly in place. The scarred man pulled his grandad even closer to him as he had more that he wanted to say to him. "I know because the woman you trapped is my mum. I know because she told me everything when I was born in the spirit world, father." He spat the final word, his anger taking over once more as he pushed his blade even further in before letting him drop to the floor.

Dropping to his knees, his grandad looked as though he was in shock. He was muttering to himself, but Arnold could not make out what it was that he was saying. Arnold felt powerless tied to the chair as he continued to try to escape and help his grandad. The lion was able to overpower the elk in its weakened state and it began to be absorbed back into his grandad.

The scarred man stood over his grandad with a look of pure hatred. "I blame you for everything. I hate you. You trapped your own wife. Do you have any idea what I have been through, what it did to me?" There wasn't just anger in the scarred man's voice, there was also a great sadness.

"I-I didn't know." His grandad raised his hand and placed it against his face and ran his fingers slowly against the scars that were gouged into his face. "You're my son?" The scarred man growled at this, burying his blade into the old man's stomach with Arnold able to see it protruding from his back. He then removed the blade and kicked him over. Arnold's grandad lay there gasping for breath, unable to talk as his mouth filled with blood. Arnold's heart sank. He could feel his heart rate racing as the anger inside consumed him. He was enraged. The scarred man had stabbed his grandad and he had been unable to help him.

"Why would you do that?" he screamed. Arnold focused on the scarred man and all he wanted was to take his blade from him and make him pay for what he had done. Someone needed to stop him before he hurt anyone else and he was determined that it was going to be him. "GET AWAY FROM HIM!" he screamed, letting go of all the rage and anger that he had built up inside him. Arnold began to give off a slight glow that illuminated the darkness around him. Feeling a strong energy flow running through him, Arnold felt energised and for a moment, his body had stopped aching and his fatigue had instantly disappeared.

A stream of light shot out from Arnold's chest as he let out all his anger and rage by screaming as hard and as loud as he could. The stream of light began to take form. Arnold looked down and saw that the energy emitting from him had slightly burnt the ropes that held him down. He pulled his arms against them and was able to break loose. Running across to his grandad he slid behind him and tried to prop him up. He was barely conscious, but Arnold was glad that he had got to him. With tears streaming down his face, he started to shake his grandad. "Come on grandad you will be ok, just keep your eyes open." The scarred man paced at a distance.

"He has had that coming for a long time. Not as satisfying as I had always dreamed but still," he snarled showing no signs of remorse for what he had just done. "He and his friends are to blame."

"You will pay for this!" Arnold shouted across, his anger and hatred there for both of them to see. Looking to his side he saw that his grandad's macahuitl blade was just within reach. He leaned over and picked it up knowing what he needed to do. He stood up to confront the scarred man who was stood just a few metres away, with his remaining lion by his side. Arnold's hand clenched tightly to the hilt of his grandad's ancient weapon.

Suddenly, a flash of light came flying between the two of them and went straight into the lion, knocking it over. It moved too fast to see what it was, but Arnold felt connected to it and knew that it was his spirit beast. The scarred man laughed and clapped his hands together.

"I told you I would help you unlock your spirit beast and I have!

You just needed the right motivation." He sneered, his face distorted with a mixture of anger and satisfaction. "Now that you have unlocked it, I am going to steal it and use it for myself. Your grandma, my mum, has a dragon spirit beast and now so will I!"

Arnold looked up at the spirit beast as it began to glide down towards him. As it came closer, he could finally see the form that it had taken. The glow around its feather's made it seem almost angelic as it silently flew down to him. Arnold smiled.

"Except you're wrong. I don't have a dragon spirit beast like my grandma had." The scarred man frowned.

"But -" He looked up in the sky and his face became contorted with rage once more.

"It's an eagle," Arnold said, proudly. The spirit beast landed next to Arnold, its large frame intimidating enough but then it spread out its wings to show an impressive wingspan that made it appear even larger. Arnold put his hand to its head and the beast lowered its crown and, in that instant, the soft glow around it appeared to soothe Arnold's anger and grief for his grandad and his mind felt clearer. His spirit beast was guiding him, and he knew he needed to follow its guidance.

"This can't be." The scarred man was infuriated. "All the signs were there; I was told you had a dragon inside you. This can't be! I need a dragon if I'm to be truly free!" he said, his anger apparent and his face distorted with blind rage. "You are of no use to me, then. Look what I did to my own dad; it is going to be easy to do the same to my nephew!"

"None of this makes any sense. Why would my grandad trap my grandma in the spirit world?" Arnold called.

"Because she was too powerful! Her spirit beast took control of her and she was too strong and dangerous. Your grandad and his friends somehow found a way of trapping her in the spirit world." The scarred man began walking towards Arnold with vengeful eyes, his dagger drawn. His lion had climbed back to its feet and ran past the scarred man as it attempted to strike out first. "The Elder, The Doyen, the Architect and the Shaman."

The eagle flew forward and began flapping its wings with

tremendous force, spraying the lion with dust, making it difficult to see. The eagle then flew at the lion with its talons and sliced the lion down its side. The lion roared and swiped at the eagle, catching its wing and sending it crashing to the floor. Arnold panicked but his spirit beast jumped back to its feet quickly and shook itself to bring all of its feathers back into place. The scarred man had reached Arnold and swiped at him with his blade, but Arnold swung the macahuitl around and was able to knock his attacker away. The macahuitl was quite heavy and the weight of it surprised Arnold, even if it was made from wood and stone. The scarred man followed with another strike which again Arnold was able to stop but then the scarred man followed with a punch with his free hand and Arnold, who had both hands on the hilt of the macahuitl, was unable to block it and took its full force in his face. He staggered backwards and the scarred man was on him straight away. He was not giving up and his intentions were clear; he wanted Arnold dead. He swung his blade at Arnold once more which Arnold stepped back to avoid. The scarred man then aimed an aerial blow towards him so Arnold grabbed hold of the top end of the macahuitl to turn it on its side to shield himself from the blow. A kick then came through the gap which took Arnold's breath away, knocking him back once more. The scarred man then jumped towards Arnold and aimed another fierce punch to his head, this time sending him crashing to the floor. Arnold was in pain but knew he needed to get back to his feet quickly if he was to survive. The scarred man was too big and too powerful for him and his combat skills far exceeded his own.

As the scarred man approached, Arnold could see the glow of his spirit beast behind him and it flew into the back of his legs knocking him to the ground. It stood in front of Arnold and placed its wings around him as if hugging him and again his pain began to fade. He got back to his feet and readied himself to face the scarred man once more. The scarred man jumped back to his feet and smiled at Arnold "Back for another hiding, boy? That takes courage and I admire that. Your spirit beast is more powerful than I gave it credit for. Maybe I will take it from you after all."

"You will have to go through me, first!" Arthur stood there with his ceremonial spear pointed at the scarred man. "You are a coward, attacking a teen and an old man." His bear ran past them and headed straight for the lion spirit beast. As the two of them began to grapple, Arnold's eagle flew towards them to give aid to the bear.

The scarred man growled before lunging at Arthur with his blade. He was quick to react to this however and pushed away his attacker but not quick enough to block the scarred man's fist that came crashing into the side of his jaw. Arnold leapt forward with the macahuitl and swung it with as much force as he could muster but the scarred man blocked this with his blade before kicking him away. He swung a blow at Arnold, but Arthur's hand came across to deflect this before the scarred man swung at him. This time Arnold blocked the attack, the scarred man's frustration building at the fluidity of their movement against him. He jumped up and landed a dropkick against the two of them, knocking them both to the floor. He quickly sprang back to his feet.

"How fitting that you shall all meet your end, here."

Arnold was quicker than his dad at getting up and he ran at the scarred man with a rage growing inside of him. He saw his dad was climbing to his feet and the scarred man was heading towards him, glaring and gripping his blade firmly in his hand. Arnold used his dad's body as a springboard and leapt through the air, swinging his macahuitl back and ready to kill him for what he had done. He swung the weapon down and crashed the hilt of the blade against the scarred man's head, sending him slamming to the floor.

At that moment, the eagle and bear smashed into the lion, knocking it back down to the floor before the grizzly stood on its hind legs and struck down with tremendous force on to the lion's back. The lion grumbled as it lay there unable to climb back to its feet due to its injuries.

"Now, now, brother," the scarred man gasped as he climbed back to his feet. "It's time you addressed me by my name. I'm Levent," he grinned. Seeing that he was outnumbered and without an active spirit beast, he stepped back towards the tower.

"Brother? What are you on about?" Arthur said, visibly confused.

"I'll let the boy fill in the gaps." He turned to the tower and stretched his arm out and the area in front of him started to distort as if looking through frosted glass. He held his dagger up to the remaining lion and it began to absorb back into the blade. Running at the distortion, he jumped towards it and then simply disappeared. Just like that, he was gone, and the distortion vanished with him.

Arnold and his dad ran at once to his grandad who lay on the ground, his breathing growing even more laboured. Arnold's eagle flew across and placed its wings over the top of him to soothe his pain as it knew that there wasn't anything else that it could do.

"I'm sorry, Arthur," Arnold's grandad gasped, as his dad cradled him in his arms. "It was the only thing we could do. She was out of control and they would have killed her."

"It doesn't matter dad it's ok. It will all be ok." His dad was rocking him, trying to soothe him the best he could, his eyes filled with tears.

"I'm proud of you son, you have raised a good boy here." He smiled at Arnold. "Pass me your hand." His grandad reached out and held Arnold's hand, placed his other hand on his chest and closed his eyes. Arnold began to feel a strange sensation as wave after wave of a gentle, pulsating feeling came over him, emanating from his grandad.

"He's transferring his auro to you," His dad explained, sniffing back the tears as he continued to comfort him. The wave got stronger and stronger and Arnold began to feel a little dizzy and nauseous, but he managed to keep it together as he knelt on the floor by his grandad's side. His auro slowly transferred over to him and his grandad smiled at Arnold and closed his eyes.

"Son, if you have something you want to say, you need to say it now," Arthur said softly. Arnold grabbed hold of his grandad's hand and moved as close as he could to his head. "I love you, grandad," was all he could muster but it was what he needed to tell him. He rested his head into his grandad's as his slow laboured breath gradually came to a stop, the pulsating sensation against his body fading until he had drifted away. Arnold had what felt like a knot in his throat and he began to sob uncontrollably. His dad wrapped his arm around him and pulled him in tightly, squeezing him as hard as he could as the two of them cried together.

"It's ok, I've got you," his dad whispered, and they sat their together as they continued to shed tears for Arnold's grandad. His grandad had gone, and Arnold had never felt grief like it.

Chapter Twenty

Arnold lay on his bed at home staring at his bedroom ceiling and thinking back on the fondest memories that he had shared with his grandad. His heart was broken. His grandad had been murdered in front of him and he had been powerless to help him.

There was a knock on his door and his dad entered with a glass of juice in one hand and a sandwich in the other. "I've brought you something to eat and drink. I know you don't feel like it, but you need to have something." He placed them next to Arnold on his bedside drawers and stood by the side of the bed as if offering Arnold the opportunity to talk, but nothing was said. He turned and began to exit the room to allow him some space.

"If only I'd been able to summon my spirit beast sooner, grandad might still be here." Arnold sat up in bed and hurriedly spat the words out; he'd had the thought in his head for the last few days.

His dad turned and walked back over to the end of his bed and sat down. "You can't think like that. Your grandad wouldn't want you to be beating yourself up over it. Levent knew what he was doing, and he knew by doing what he did that kind of emotional response would

186

trigger your spirit beast." His dad stood up and reached into his pocket, pulled something out and passed it to him.

Taking it from his dad, he saw that it was an old torn photo and Arnold instantly recognised what it was.

"We found that inside the tower. No doubt it was deliberately left there for us."

"I know - this is grandma. I've seen the other half of the photo at grandad's house." It was strange finally seeing her after all this time in an old black and white photo. There she was with her beautiful smile, long dark hair and shining eyes. Her hand rested just below her stomach as if she was cradling it, and to her side was a small child that must have been his dad, holding her hand tightly.

"Did you know?" Arnold pressed, "about what happened?"

"No, I didn't. I barely remember anything from that time and dad always told me he didn't have any photos of her." His dad looked saddened as he thought about his parents. Even though he was an adult with his own family he was now an orphan in some sense as he no longer had a parent in this world. He looked up at Arnold. "You said that both your grandad and Levent mentioned that she had a dragon spirit beast and that this corrupted her."

"Yes," Arnold replied. His dad nodded.

"Corruption does not happen often but when it does, you lose that person. The spirit beast takes over and they are not in control," he explained.

"So, grandma was a prisoner?" Arnold asked. Again, his dad nodded.

"It was no one's fault what happened to her. Corruption is out of anyone's control."

"How did they trap her in the spirit world?" Arnold was eager to understand.

"That is the million pound question. I have no idea. No one does because it has never been done before." His dad reached across and took back the old photo from Arnold and gazed lovingly at the picture of his grandma. "At least with this picture we now have something to remember her by." He stood up from the bed and again began to exit the room placing the photograph back in his pocket. Arnold got up from his bed as he had more questions. "What about Otto, what will happen to him?"

"He doesn't remember what happened, he was found unconscious on the floor. However, Sue is dead, and it was his shield that did it. He will not face trial as I can evidence that she attacked us, however, he has taken a life which means that he will no longer be able to train at the Chichen."

"What?" Arnold began to protest but it was no use. The decision had already been made and there was nothing he could do about it.

"Please always remember, capture not kill. If we kill those that wrong us, then we are no better than them." With that, he left the room and closed the door behind him.

Arnold fell back to his bed wondering about Otto, wishing there was something he could do for him. He picked up his phone and sent him a text, but he wasn't holding out for a reply. Otto hadn't replied to any of Arnold's messages since the confrontation at the tower. Arnold ate the sandwich that his dad had brought him and had a drink of his juice before he lay back down on his bed. He wished his grandad was still here, he wished his friend would reply to him so that he could say sorry for how he had been, and he wished to see his uncle again so that he could avenge what he had done.

Arnold was free and soaring high. The sensation was amazing, and it energised every part of his body. For the first few days following his grandad's death, he could not sleep but now he was having his dreams about flying again. The air pressing against him was refreshing, like jumping in a cold pool on a hot day. He could feel the sharpness of the wind against him and the chill that came with it but all the while having the warmth of the sun against his body. He was high up and he was in full control; since learning that his spirit beast was an eagle his dreams had felt even more vivid, even more real and the connection between the two of them was strong. The eagle inside him had given him the strength to do the right thing against Levent on the night he killed his grandad. It had calmed his temper so that he could think clearer rather than acting on impulse. In his dream Arnold was in control and could fly in whichever direction he wanted, having got used to his eagle body he could soar as high as he wanted, glide as fast as he wanted and most importantly stop when he wanted. He loved having the control of battling against each gust of wind as it tried to halt his progress and he liked learning how to dive bomb and pull up at the last second giving him a spike of adrenaline like he had never felt before.

On this occasion, he was simply gliding, letting the wind do all the work for him. Riding each gust like a surfer in the ocean. There was a knack to it as flying was an art form and he was learning to really enjoy it. Whilst flying, Arnold realised that he recognised the area below and that he had been here before. He looked across the fields below and saw the tower at Rivington, the difference being that this tower did not look old, weary or unkempt. The area around the tower was not overgrown. The trees and woodlands around it looked healthy, so perfect in fact that it looked like an artist had drawn them. Tilting his wing so that he could glide down to the tower to get a closer look he began to steadily lower himself at a safe pace and keeping a safe distance. He began to circle the tower as he drew closer to see if he could see anything through the tower's windows using his eagle-eyed vision. He could and as he glided closer, he could make out two people in conversation. One was Levent, his scarred face unmistakable. The other took Arnold a few moments to recognise. Levent was talking to a young woman with long dark hair and shining eyes and she looked younger than Levent. She looked pretty much the same as the photograph he had held in his hand recently. It was his grandma. He continued to circle, watching from afar until he realised that the two of them had stopped talking. Arnold's grandma had turned to face him and looked directly in his eyes.

He knew at this moment that she knew that he was there.

He knew at this moment that his grandma was still alive.

Arnold will return in

The Eagle and the Jaguar

Made in the USA
Middletown, DE
16 November 2020

24237310R00118